P9-DEQ-728

# The
# RIVER
## and the
# BOOK

## Frankston City Libraries

Please return items by the date printed on your loans docket.
Please report any damage to staff. Fees are charged for items
returned late. To renew loans by phone, quote your library
card number or go to **library.frankston.vic.gov.au**

| **FRANKSTON LIBRARY** | **CARRUM DOWNS LIBRARY** | **SEAFORD LIBRARY** |
|---|---|---|
| 60 Playne Street, Frankston. | 203 Lyrebird Drive, Carrum Downs. | Corner Station & Broughton Streets, Seaford. |
| Ph: 9784 1020 | Ph: 8773 9539 | Ph: 9784 1048 |

## Other titles by this author

# The
# RIVER
## and the
# BOOK

## ALISON CROGGON

**WALKER
BOOKS**

*For Catherine Dan, with gratitude and thanks*

This is a work of fiction. Names, characters, places and incidents are either the product of the author's imagination or, if real, used fictitiously. All statements, activities, stunts, descriptions, information and material of any other kind contained herein are included for entertainment purposes only and should not be relied on for accuracy or replicated as they may result in injury.

First published in Great Britain 2015 by Walker Books Ltd
87 Vauxhall Walk, London SE11 5HJ

2 4 6 8 10 9 7 5 3 1

Text © 2015 Alison Croggon
Cover and chapter illustrations © 2015 Katie Harnett

Translation from Mahmoud Darwish's poem "Mural" by Sargon Boulus, originally published in Banipal 15/16 (Spring, 2003), reprinted here courtesy of Banipal

The right of Alison Croggon and Katie Harnett to be identified as author and illustrator of this work respectively has been asserted by them in accordance with the Copyright, Designs and Patents Act 1988

This book has been typeset in Palatino

Printed and bound in Great Britain by Clays Ltd, St Ives plc

All rights reserved. No part of this book may be reproduced, transmitted or stored in an information retrieval system in any form or by any means, graphic, electronic or mechanical, including photocopying, taping and recording, without prior written permission from the publisher.

British Library Cataloguing in Publication Data:
a catalogue record for this book is available from the British Library

ISBN 978-1-4063-5602-1 (UK)
ISBN 978-1-925081-72-5 (Australia)

www.walker.co.uk
www.walkerbooks.com.au

T CROG
18735035
(AUST)
(Fantasy)

*O my name: where are we now?*
*Tell me: What is now? What is tomorrow?*
*What's time, what's place, what's old, what's new?*

*One day we shall become what we want.*

From "Mural", by Mahmoud Darwish, translated by
Sargon Boulos

1

I am not a storyteller, so I don't know how to begin. When I think of Blind Harim the Storyteller, my courage wavers. Harim's voice enters your blood like a drug, bringing visions and strange dreams. He attracts crowds of people who bring mats and sit around him in rows, their faces upraised like flowers. The men roll cigarettes of dark tobacco and smoke them as they gaze at the ground, their harsh faces suddenly gentle, and the women bring bags of sugared almonds and pop them into the mouths of small children, to keep them quiet.

Mely and I go to listen to Harim when the city seems too bright and cruel, too full of noise. Behind the neon signs and glass skyscrapers of the car-choked streets, behind the pavements flooded with businessmen in suits and wealthy high-heeled women and beggars and window-washers and tourists whose sunglasses reflect the entire world in miniature, far behind them, where no tourist ever goes, there is a market where people come to buy and sell. There you can buy cucumbers and second-hand mobile phones, engine parts and

7

spices, dull-eyed fish caught in the stinking harbour and iridescent beetles in boxes, patched clothes and old shoes. Nothing
costs very much, because everyone who goes there is poor. But
nobody is too poor to listen to a story.

When Harim arrives at the market, people turn and stare in
his wake, although there doesn't seem to be anything special
about him. He is led by a small boy, who carries his cushion
and then sits silently beside him as he speaks. I have never
heard the boy say a single word.

There is one dusty tree in the square, which offers some thin
shade against the sun. That is where Harim tells his stories.
He bends down slowly, feeling his way down the trunk with
the tips of his fingers. He lifts his sightless eyes to the sunlight
that filters through the branches and rests his stick across his
knees, and then, very carefully, rolls out an old, worn piece of
embroidered silk, which he places on the ground before him.
That cloth is where you put your coins when he has finished
telling his story.

He waits for the correct time to begin. Somehow he senses
when it is right, when a sufficient crowd has gathered but
before the people have become impatient. Most of the time he
tells us stories we already know, but sometimes he tells a new
story that nobody has ever heard. I like the new ones best. He
always begins in the same way: *As far away as the North Wind,
and as long ago as for ever…* And when he says those words, the
crowd holds its breath, and then everyone sighs out, all at once.
Mely curls up in my lap and begins to purr. I look around at
the others, and I know my face is the same as theirs: bright and
hungry. In that moment we are all children, and the world is
fresh and full of promise.

I am not a storyteller like Harim, but my story burns inside
me, wanting to be told, and I have decided to write it down.
I am sitting in my kitchen at my table. It is evening, and the

moths are fluttering around the room, bumping into my lamp. Mely is fast asleep on the other chair. I like the noise the pen makes as it scratches across the paper. It is very peaceful. It feels like a proper time to begin.

This is the story of the River and the Book, but it is my story too.

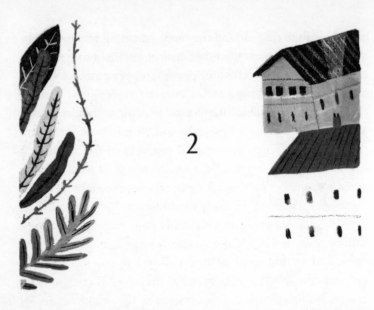

2

My name is Simbala Da Kulafir Atan Mucarek Abaral Effenda Nuum. It's usually shortened to Simbi Nuum, but those who love me call me Sim.

Once, not very long ago, I lived in a village with my father and my brothers and sisters and cousins and uncles and aunts. My father, Dato, is a fisherman, and I have two brothers, Tiak and Solman, and three sisters, Shiha, Ketsi and Little Beran. They are a noisy, mischievous tribe. Compared to my siblings, I was considered a solemn child. Perhaps it is because I am the oldest, but my mother said I was born serious.

My village is a small, unremarkable place like many others that line the River. Its name is not important, except to me. There are perhaps three dozen houses. They are the humble colours of the earth we live on, pink and brown and umber, built many years ago by hands that now sleep in the same earth they shaped with such love. The walls are thick and the windows small, and the houses make flat planes of light and shade that catch every mood of the seasons. The doors are wooden and painted blue or red, and they invite you inside, into their hearts.

Inside you blink with the sudden colour: there are big cushions as vivid as blood, and bright embroidered hangings, and the glowing wood of low tables smooth with long use. Pierced brass lamps sway from the beams and throw their intricate shadows over whitewashed walls and thick carpets, which are patterned like the gardens full of peacocks in the stories my grandmother told me. And always the smells of food cooking and the sounds of people talking or arguing or laughing.

When I was a child I never went hungry. Each year we harvested a crop of barley, and my father grew cabbages, radishes, turnips, peas, beets and beans, and we had a small orchard of apple and walnut trees, with a mulberry tree to sweeten our table and mountain pepper to spice our dishes. There was meat and milk and, of course, fish. Sheep and pigs wandered in the street, and chickens scratched for grain next to the black-headed cranes that came each summer. No one ever chased the cranes away: they were welcome guests, the messengers of the gods. Each spring, when my grandmother saw the first crane winging towards the village, she smiled and raised her arms in blessing, and quoted the poet: *Watch for the cranes, who will bring my love to you, even as far as the Plains of Pembar.*

I didn't know the rest of that poem for many years, and when at last I heard all of it, I wept. By then I was far from the Plains of Pembar, and my love was bruised and sad in my chest. And now when I look up and see the cranes high overhead, their necks stretched before them as they beat their way forward on their long migration, I ask them to carry my love with them, to those who love me and call me Sim.

# 3

In our village we had two treasures: the River, which was our road and our god; and the Book, which was our history, our oracle and our soul.

The River shaped our lives. It was a fact, like the ground and the sky, and so we didn't think about it: the River was just there, surly or generous, gentle or deadly. In winter it ran fast and narrow, too fast to freeze over, although sometimes you saw chunks of ice swirling in the currents. In summer it swelled with the melt from the faraway snows, and ran slow and brown. Every few years it rose above its banks and spilled over our fields, spreading black, pungent silt that fertilized abundant harvests. It gave us fish and drinking water and cleaned our clothes and our bodies, and we siphoned off its waters to feed our fields and orchards through a network of canals. Sometimes it played with us, a clear, laughing spirit, and sometimes it turned savage and drowned us.

We all knew that the River flowed from the mountains, which curled beneath the western rim of the world. It was said that our village was founded many generations ago by people who had fled war and famine in the lands on the far side of the mountains. I sometimes wondered what had made them stop there, what made them decide to build their homes at just that bend on the River. Was it because they were tired and wanted to walk no further? Or did something call out to them from the land, an omen that said to them, *Here is where you can make your home*: a bright wren singing in a bush, perhaps, or a rainbow? When I asked the Book, it simply said: *Every where is here*. I puzzled over that for days, but I couldn't make any sense of it.

In our village, no one in living memory had ever seen the mountains. There was no reason to go west; that way there were only the Upper Plains, with a few small villages like our own clinging to the River. Adventurers went east, towards the cities. It seemed miraculous to me, who lived on the plains with horizons stretching out on every side as far as the eye could see, that there could be such things as mountains. I studied the pictures in the Book and tried to imagine what they were like, and all my childhood I dreamed of going there. The Book told me that in the centre of the mountain range is a great peak with four sides facing north, south, east and west, and down each face flow the four rivers that feed the world. Our River flows from the eastern side. This mountain is the birth chair of the gods and it holds up the sky. It is called Yntara, which means *She* in the old language: the mother, the goddess. The Book said that if ever the four rivers died, it would be the end of the world.

The River was our road: it brought business and news. In the warm months the trader Mizan chugged upstream in his brightly painted barge. He sold dark sea salt, cinnamon, cloves and almond oil, black tea, steel knives and pots, minerals for the dye-makers and trinkets and perfumes for our pleasure, and he bought the fine cloth we wove from sheep wool through the long, cold winters.

The only city people who bothered to make the long journey to our village were the tax collector and the trader. Mizan's visit was always an occasion for a feast. The tax collector was feasted as well, but no one trusted him because he had a thin, sour face and demanded our money. (I sometimes wondered if his work made him sour, since no one ever welcomed him with pleasure, and I felt a little sorry for him.) Mizan was considered an honourable man. He had thighs as thick as tree trunks and a barrel chest, and his fat, friendly face was scarred by pox. He was widely respected for his hard-bargaining, his gargantuan appetite and his huge laugh. He would sit between my father and grandmother, an honoured guest of the household, and in exchange for our hospitality he would tell us news of the cities of the east.

Often the news was of war and unrest, and the adults would talk in low voices, their faces dark and serious. At those times there were fewer coins to hoard in the chest where we kept our precious things, but otherwise these events were far away and scarcely affected us. Whether the news was bad or good, it seemed to us children to be as unreal as tales of a legendary past, *as long ago as for ever*. It had nothing to do with us.

Nobody knew when our River had begun to fail. Some said the warnings had been there before I was born, but they were so slow, so gradual, that nobody really noticed. After all, the River had its moods, and sometimes it was less generous, sometimes more. The first sign was the disappearance of the summer floods that enriched our fields. The usual cycle was every three years, give or take a year or two: in times of wealth the River could flood two or three years in a row; in times of poverty it crept between its banks and refused to overflow at all. The longest period without flooding in living memory was eight years, during a terrible drought in my grandmother's girlhood.

When the River had not flooded for six years, she shook her head and said the dry times were coming again.

I was ten years old then. I remember that the spring prayers that year were long and solemn, and my father bought some special incense to burn at the temple. But the River didn't flood that year, nor the year after, nor the year after that, no matter how fervent our prayers nor how rich our incense.

We could still irrigate our fields, and we fed the soil as best we could, but without the floods, our harvests were poorer than they had been. As people do, we adjusted to the new conditions, and things went on as they had before.

Then we began to notice that the level of the River was falling, bit by bit, year after year. Again it was almost imperceptible: but the high-water marks went steadily down and down.

I was too busy to worry about the River. I had just turned fifteen, the age at which I became a grown woman. My father presented me to the temple with the other girls and boys my age, and we had the spring celebrations – a feast with singing and dancing that went on for three days. I was proud and happy, because I now had the right to marry if I wished to, and I could mark the cloth I wove with my own initials and make some money for myself. I was planning to buy some silk for a new dress when Mizan came that summer, and perhaps a necklace. And at last I was an Effenda, a Keeper of the Book.

# 4

Inside the Book was written everything that had been, everything that was and everything that was to come.

The task of my family was the Keeping. That is the story of my name: among my people, your name says who you are and where you are from. It tells my mother's name, Kulafir, and my grandmother's, Atan, and my great-grandmother's, Mucarek, and my great-great-grandmother's, Abaral; and it says we are all the Keepers of the Nuum, the Book. The Book was passed down from mother to daughter, and it had been that way for longer than anyone could remember. It was so, and it had always been so, and no one thought that it would ever be any different.

The Book was kept in a plain wooden box that was as old as the Book itself. The wood was dark, hard and grainless, polished with the use of many hands, so you could no longer tell what kind of tree it was made from. Only the Keepers had the right to open the box and take out the Book. It would never have occurred to anyone in the village to violate that law. We kept it in a windowless room that opened off the kitchen. The room was just big enough for a low table and long cushions, and a lamp always burned there. The Book stood on a deep shelf set into the wall furthest from the door.

If anyone in the village had a question that they couldn't answer, they would ask the Book. Should Istan marry Loki, who was very handsome but owned no sheep, or should she marry Sopili, who had a harelip but owned a dozen sheep and three fields? Should Foolish Dipli spend his life savings on an engine for his fishing boat? Will Iranu's son ever return from the city in the east? When will the drought end, when will the River flood again? Will the drought ever end?

"Sometimes they will ask things that make you want to smile," my grandmother told me once. "But you must never mock or belittle anyone who comes to ask the knowledge of the Book. They may seem small or petty concerns, but if a person is moved to ask something of the Book, it means it matters to them. It is not for the Keeper to judge. And you must never break a confidence. Any question asked of the Book, no matter what it is, is secret. You will find that more difficult than you expect."

I began to learn how to read the Book when I was five years old. My mother was still alive then, and she gave me my first lesson. She washed me with scented oil and braided my hair as if we were to attend a ceremony at the temple. Then she lifted the heavy cloth that hung over the doorway and led me into the room where the Book was kept. I often played there; it was not forbidden to anyone, unless a visitor had come to ask a question. I liked it, because it was the most peaceful room in the house. On the table was a wooden doll I had left behind that very morning.

That afternoon it seemed to be a different place, a place where I had never been before. I held my breath as my mother

17

took the Book from the shelf and out of its box and placed it on the table. She carefully lifted the plain, heavy cover and opened it out, and I saw the yellow pages and the black and red lettering for the first time. I reached out and touched the pages. It felt like touching something alive. I had never seen anything so beautiful.

"You will learn how to read this," said my mother. "It will take your whole life, and you will never reach the end. And each time you open it, it will be as if you are opening it for the first time."

I looked at the writing. There were no gaps between the letters and they ran down the page, line after line, in a heavy block. Every now and then there was a red letter among the black, like a flower in a field of dark earth.

"What does it say?" I asked.

"It is a poem. A very old poem. But it is always new." My mother turned a page, and revealed a picture. I snuggled up close to her, so I could look at it. It was a drawing of a woman seated at a table next to a little girl. They were both reading a book. The woman looked like my mother, and the girl looked like me. The more I stared at the drawing, the more like us it was: there was even a doll lying on the table.

There was writing underneath, and I asked my mother what it said.

"It says: *Kulafir begins to teach Simbala the secrets of the Book,*" she said.

I don't remember being surprised or afraid to see a picture of myself in a book that was older than I could imagine. I think I was pleased. But for many years after my mother died I searched for that drawing. Although I leafed through every single page over and over, I never found it again.

5

Once I lived in a place where I knew the name for everything. Now I live in a city that is full of new things. If I went back to my village tomorrow – if my village is still there as I remember it – and tried to tell my family about what I have seen, they would wrinkle their brows, they would be perplexed. They would try to understand, because they are courteous, but what I told them would be beyond their comprehension. They would think, like I did when I was a child listening to the traders, that I was telling them marvellous fables.

I am not sure that I understand the city very well. I am still an outsider; I am still learning the rules and the words. The knowledge I spent so many hard years learning has no place here. In any case, not many people are interested. My knowledge comes from the old life, the backward and ignorant world of peasants. To understand takes too much time, and who has time? Nobody has any time.

Sometimes it seems to me that those who are interested, the foreigners who do have time, are the worst of all. They think that the things I know are exotic and strange, and my knowledge excites them. They treat me like some kind of priestess. The more I try to explain, the more their imaginations fatten and distort. They wear our clothes and decorate their houses with our gods, and they learn enough of our language to order food from a hawker and to observe the cruder courtesies, and they burn incense as if they lived in temples. They think knowledge is something you can buy, and I often wonder why they come to me instead of consulting the sages of their own lands. If I didn't know better, I would think that they do not have sages of their own.

Sometimes it frightens me to look into their eyes. It is as if a hard barrier divides their soul from themselves. Their soul cries like a lost child deep inside them, but all they hear is a faint echo of its sobbing. They can't break down the barrier and take its hand and comfort it, because they don't even know that the barrier is there. They only know that they are unhappy, and they believe that happiness is something that can be found, and that when they find it, it will solve everything.

On the other hand, as Mely likes to remind me when I complain too much, these people are the reason why I am not so poor that I have to live in a shack made of boxes. They pay me generously. I try not to be ungrateful, and I try to remember my grandmother's admonition that one should not mock the desires or questions of others, no matter how trivial or stupid they might seem. I deal with them as honestly as I can, but I know I cannot give them what they want. A gift must be received as well as given, a poem must be listened to with the ears of the soul, and their souls are crying so hard they can hear nothing. They make me feel like a fraud, and I begin to doubt myself. I wonder whether my whole life is a dream, a story I made up and began to believe because I told it so often.

When I feel poisoned by their strange hunger, I catch a bus

to the west, to the shantytown, and walk around the market and listen to the storyteller. I speak to the people who live on the edges, the poor who come from villages far away. They do not talk about what they have lost, because it is too painful, because they have not found the words to say it, because there is no need, because everyone has lost the same things. Sometimes they are coarse and brutal and selfish because they have lost so much, because they no longer even hope, but I do not despise them for that. More often they are kind and generous. They sing the old poems, and they eat out of the common bowl, and in a corner of their shack there is always a shrine to the small gods, even if it is made of scraps of paper and wood and tinfoil. Their children are sharp and bright, and when they grow up, many of them do not keep the gods in their houses. What use are our gods in a big city where no one listens? I think that if they forget their gods they may forget themselves, like so many of the foreigners who visit me: but how can I blame them for that?

The shanty dwellers do not come from my village. Many of them don't even speak my language. They are caught between one world and another, and they no longer belong anywhere. When I go to visit them, I feel less alone.

# 6

When I told Mely I wanted to write down my story, at first she said nothing. She stared at me with her cool green eyes and I thought she was laughing at me. At last she flicked her tail. "Why not?" she said. "You are a Keeper. You should have a Book. And you might as well make your own."

Mely's comment took me aback. I hadn't thought of my story as being like the Book, and it seemed disrespectful to think that I could replace the Book with my own words. I wondered then if perhaps I shouldn't write it, if to do so would be a kind of blasphemy. When I told Mely my thoughts, she flicked her tail again. "You people are strange," she said. "Someone must have made the Book. It didn't leap out of a burrow or fall off a tree. So why can't you make one too?"

"But I don't want to replace the Book," I said. "I just want to write down my story."

"So? It will be a new Book," said Mely. She was already bored with the conversation. "I'm tired of looking for the old one."

And so I went to the paper shop in my street and bought

a notebook and a pen. The notebook has black covers and creamy white paper with faint blue lines, and the pen has black ink. They were expensive, but it seemed important to buy the proper materials for such a solemn undertaking as writing a new Book.

I put the pen and the notebook on my table in the kitchen. I left them there for days. I didn't have the courage to make the first mark on the paper, to sully that perfect creamy-white field with my handwriting.

"What if I make a mistake?" I asked Mely.

"How will you know if it's a mistake?"

"I don't know anything about stories," I said. "I will make lots of mistakes."

I knew it was stupid to ask Mely. What does a cat know about books? But she said, "How can you make a mistake? It's your story." And then she fell asleep at once, so I couldn't ask her any more questions.

That night I opened the notebook and began my story. I have been writing it now for six evenings, and every morning I read what I have written to Mely, because I need to feel I am making it for someone. I know I am not telling things in the proper order, but I think Mely is right: it is my story, so I can't make a mistake.

And tonight I am remembering how I would walk out of the house at dawn on spring mornings, my feet bare and freezing, because I loved to see the sun on the dew drops that hung trembling from each grass blade.

I thought that the dew on the grass at sunrise was like a sultan's jewels in one of my grandmother's stories. When she spoke of vast treasures, of vaults heaped with diamonds and rubies, I always imagined the dew at the moment when the sun's first rays spilled over the horizon and struck it into fiery brilliance. I would stare at them until my eyes were dazzled and

23

warm tears ran down my cheeks. I could smell the woodsmoke as people started their fires for the first meal of the day, and I listened to the low bleat of the sheep and the quiet music of the River and the early cries of the birds.

My tracks stretched dark behind me where my feet had pressed down the grey, wet grasses, and on the slope in front of me sparkled a miraculous carpet stitched with countless tiny gems, each one a polished and perfect crystal that flashed emerald and violet and ruby and gold. It was so beautiful I held my breath. And then the sun lifted and the magic faded, and I realized that the numbness of my feet was climbing up my legs and making me shiver, and I turned back to the house and the duties of the day.

On the morning after my mother's funeral, I went out of the house before dawn to be on my own. I wasn't thinking about the dew. I just wanted to be alone. The day before the house had been so full of people. The whole village had come to pay its respects, as well as village heads from up and down the River, and we had many guests sleeping in the house. My mother had been an important woman. All day I had gravely accepted their gifts and their sympathy, and I worried about how to serve the lamb and whether Raitam was burning the bread, and who was sitting where. Dipli and Lokaran might come to blows if they sat at the same table, but I didn't want to offend either of them by giving the other precedence, and the Juta family was feuding but, while everyone knew about the feud, nobody was certain who was on whose side because the alliances and enmities changed every day… And underneath I thought I would suffocate with impatience and anger that I had to think of these things at all, which had always been the cares of my mother. I knew my grandmother was really in charge – she moved quietly and deftly between the guests, her face calm like iron – but I knew that now it was my job too, and

I worried about everything. I kept my face formal and courteous as was required of the Effenda, and my stomach grew hot and tight with rage.

When everything was finished, when the last lament had been sung and the keeners had taken their bells and cymbals and gone home, I fell into bed like a stone. I slept badly. All night I dreamed I was in the River, the waters hammering against my ears until I couldn't tell whether the noise was the water or the pulse of my own blood. I held my breath and held my breath, my chest burning with the pressure of the black water, and then surfaced out of the dream like a drowning swimmer, gasping, and then, because I was too exhausted to resist it, slid back into the endless, suffocating dark.

I woke up properly when it was still dark. I could hear my sisters breathing beside me, and in the next room my grandmother snorted in her sleep and turned over. I felt as tired as if I hadn't slept at all, but I suddenly couldn't bear to stay in bed, I couldn't bear to be in this house with all these people, breathing the same stale, stuffy air. I slipped out of bed, threw a sheepskin coat over my nightdress and stole out of the house. Once I was outside I walked down to the River, which ran faintly luminous between its banks. The sky was just beginning to lighten towards sunrise.

I sat down on a flat stone and waited. I don't really know what I was waiting for, but I think I half expected to see my mother walking up from the house to call me in, as she did sometimes when I went out early. I watched as the stars faded and the landscape began to materialize out of the night and become solid again, and the rim of the world grew rose-pink and deepened to orange and then split with molten gold, and the first rays of the sun speared the wide, empty plains. And as I watched, the carpet of gems flared before me. Their cold brilliance hurt me, and their beauty filled me with anger.

My mother had not come. My mother had not come, and the sun had risen, and I knew she would never come now, she would never call me again. And I knocked the jewels off the grasses, all the dew drops I could reach, so their prisms smashed into dull wetness. I tore the grasses until they cut my hands, I fell down on my face and howled in the heartless chill of the grey and empty morning.

7

My mother died the winter after I was presented at the temple. If she had been sickening, if there had been some warning, it might have been a little easier to bear. It seemed that one day she was there – scolding us when we squabbled, or sighing patiently and standing to greet a villager who was holding a squawking chicken by the feet as payment for his question, or leaning forward in the morning to light the fire in the stove, her plaited hair swinging over her sleep-blurred face – and then the next she had just vanished. She died of a fierce fever. She went out one bad night to help a young woman suffering in childbed, and a storm caught her as she walked home and chilled her to the bone.

I don't remember anything about the next days. I have not one single image of the sickbed, of my brothers and sisters crying, of Grandmother burning herbs in a dish and chanting, not one memory of my mother gasping for breath, of her skin burning, of her raving when her fever took hold. My grandmother told me what happened, because I asked her to, and she also

27

told me that I was there beside the bed all the time, and that I did not sleep for those two days. But I can't remember anything at all.

The woman my mother had gone to help lived through her trouble, and so did her baby. For many months I couldn't meet the woman's eyes when I saw her and I hated her son, because together they had killed my mother. I have long forgiven them, and prayed for them to forgive me for hating them so much. "The gods give and take in their own time," said my grandmother. "There is no profit in assigning fault." She was correct, of course, but at the time it was hard not to blame them. I missed my mother so much. And after she died, the house felt different: a light went out, a soft illumination I had never noticed until it was gone.

My father's face closed like a fist. He had always been a quiet man, but now he rarely spoke at all, and sometimes the baffled desolation and anger in his face frightened us. He had loved my mother from the first moment he saw her, when he was a young boatman from the next village. He had come downriver to do some trading and my mother was on the riverbank washing clothes. He told us that it was a dull day, with heavy slate-coloured clouds brooding overhead, but my mother shone with a light that seemed to come from her skin, and as the water splashed up around her strong arms it seemed to be made of liquid silver. He stared, transfixed, as the current pulled his boat around the river bend, and when she was out of sight he wondered whether he had dreamed her, or if she was a goddess who had appeared in human form, as they were said to do. But then he saw her in the village and asked her name, and that very afternoon he brought a courting gift to our house and asked permission to woo her, and the following spring they were married.

When we were small, we often begged to hear that story.

And sometimes, smiling in his quiet way, my father would tell it, and as he did his eyes would meet my mother's, and then they would both smile.

# 8

The omens, it was said later, were bad that year. In the spring-time, a crane crashed into our chimney and broke its neck. My grandmother saw it happen and ran up to help the stricken bird, but it was already dead, its long neck twisted grotesquely under its wings. She picked up the heavy body, which was still quivering with the life that had just left it, and there were tears in her eyes. It was the second time I had seen her weep in less than a month, although before that year I had never seen her cry at all. She buried the crane without saying a word to the children who watched her, curious and frightened, and then she went into the room with the Book and shut the door, and she didn't come out for a long time. When she did emerge, she looked much older, as if something inside her had been quenched. I was too afraid to ask her what she had read, although I was the only person in the family who had the right to ask.

The floods did not come in the summer, which meant it was twelve years since the River had last overrun its banks. There had never been such a gap before. Many people now said that the floods would never come again. Even without them, the River had always swelled in summer, rising greedily up its banks. This summer, the River shrank. Its level sank more than the length of a man's arm below its lowest-ever point, and its waters were browner and murkier. Its voice changed: it was shallower and more urgent, like the voice of a sick man.

It was less than a month after the crane broke its neck on our chimney that we first heard of the water wars upriver. It happened this way. I was lighting the fire before first light when Foolish Dipli came to the door. He knocked and then waited for me to finish my task, squatting patiently by the step. It was very early for questions and Grandmother was still abed, so I took my time. When I came outside, he stood up and smiled apologetically.

"They need help," he said, and pointed towards the River.

"Who?" I asked, a little impatient.

"Some strangers from upriver," said Dipli. "A woman and a baby and a man. They need help." He smiled again, but this time I noticed the expression in his eyes. Something was very wrong.

I swallowed hard and followed him quickly down to the riverbank. The sun was only just edging over the horizon and its gold light fell on a small boat drawn up on the bank. It was crammed with all sorts of things – pots, sacks of barley, clothes, an oil lamp, blankets – all thrown in higgledy-piggledy. The boat was so full I wondered that it hadn't sunk in the River. A thin, exhausted-looking man was sitting on the bank, holding a sleeping baby, and in the boat lay a woman.

I could see that the woman was badly injured. Her dress was stained with dried blood all down her left side. She lay with her eyes closed, and her breath was loud and laboured. A hot panic began to beat in my stomach. I thought that I should go back to the house and get my grandmother, but Dipli was watching

31

me, trusting that I would know what to do.

I looked to the man for permission, and then climbed into the boat and picked up the woman's hand. It was as cold as the river water. As I touched her, her body arched violently and she made a harsh noise in her throat. Fresh blood broke out and dripped on the blanket where she was lying. And then I felt something pass me, as if a bird whirred past my ear, and I knew she was dead, even before the last of her breath whistled out of her throat.

I remembered then that I was an Effenda. I leant forward and closed her eyes, and I blessed the soul that had just flown away. I saw, with some other part of me, that my hands were trembling. Then I realized the man was standing at my shoulder. He said nothing at all. He touched the woman's brow with the tips of his fingers, and turned away, holding the baby tightly to his breast.

I scrambled out of the boat. "You should come to the house," I said.

He turned towards me and I met his eyes. They were like two holes in his face; they seemed to be looking at nothing. My mouth went dry, and I could say nothing more. I had never seen such pain in a man's expression, not even in my father after my mother died.

Dipli gently grasped the man's arm and led him back to our house. And there my grandmother took the baby from his unresisting arms and fed it some warm sheep's milk. She brought him some soup and stood over him until he had eaten the whole bowl. Then she filled a basin with rainwater and gave him dry, clean clothes, and she led him to the top room, where we housed our guests. When she had taken care of the living, she went down to the riverbank to see to the dead.

On the way, Grandmother went to see Sulihar, who had given birth a week earlier, and asked if she would wet-nurse

32

the baby. The boy was very small, no older than a month, and he was starving, which was why he lay so limp and quiet. And Sulihar, who had no shortage of milk in her enormous breasts and loved all infant creatures, took the baby and cared for him.

The stranger slept all that day and all night. Late the next morning, he rose from his bed and came downstairs. He was wearing the clean clothes Grandmother had given him, and he had washed himself. The day before you couldn't really tell what age he was; he looked shrunken and tired, and he was covered in grime. Now you could see that he was a young man, maybe not many years older than I was.

He told us that his name was Kular Minuar, and that he came from a village a long way upriver. The woman who had died was his wife, Ilino Av'hardar, and the baby boy was called Inhiral Minuar. They had been travelling on the River for days without coming to shore. Even though his wife was so badly hurt, he hadn't dared to stop.

My grandmother nodded gravely, and then told him that he could tell us anything he wanted to later, but that now he should eat. He smiled tiredly, as if her words reminded him of someone he knew, and he sat down at the table and obediently ate the beans she served him. She then asked him if he would like to see his baby and his wife. He nodded, and she took him first to Sulihar and then to the temple where she had laid out the body, ready for the cremation. She came back alone, her mouth set firmly, and wouldn't tell us anything except that Kular would come back when he wanted to. There was a fierce glint in her eyes that forbade further questions, and all of us worked with our heads down that afternoon, because she picked fault with the smallest things.

By evening, the house smelt delicious: we had spent the afternoon cooking a stew of mutton and turnips, and there was new bread to dip in the dark salt and oil on the table, and fresh greens. My father, who had been away downriver for a few days, returned just before twilight, and we welcomed him home and told him what had happened. Just when we had finished our tale, Kular knocked at the door and entered. His face was as hard as stone, and again his eyes were empty. He no longer seemed like a young man. I couldn't look at him, because it made me feel ashamed that I did not know how to help.

My father greeted him and asked him if he would like to eat with us. Then he looked closely at Kular's face, in the way that I hadn't dared to. "Or, if you are not well," he said, "I can get Sim to bring some food to your room."

It was not like my father to be so thoughtful, but my mother had not long died, and perhaps he saw his own grief in Kular's face. Kular hesitated, staring down at the floor, and I thought for a moment that he would choose to be alone. But then he looked up and met my father's eye, and said that he would be honoured to eat with us.

So we ate a good meal together, and then my sister Shiha played the *tar*, the five-stringed lute, with which she has some skill, and she sang the song of the lovesick minstrel, her husky voice rising sweet and pure:

*Let my love embrace you,*
*Your black eyes and eyebrows, Jira.*
*I burn with longing for you,*
*Cure me of this fever, Jira.*
*Let the partridge cackle*
*Like old women, Jira.*
*They cannot see into my heart.*
*Only you can see me, Jira.*

It had been one of my mother's favourite songs, and I hadn't heard it sung since she died. I stole a look at my father, but his

34

face was blank and inscrutable. The young man was listening with his hands shading his eyes, and when he looked up, his eyes were bright in the golden lamplight. He stood then, awkwardly twisting his hands as he struggled to speak, looking around at our upturned faces. At last he said, "Thank you. I had forgotten people could be kind." Then he sat down and turned his face into the shadows. Grandmother sharply chided Tiak, who was pulling Shiha's hair, but I knew it was to give Kular time to recover, because he was in tears.

The *tar* was put away, and the smaller children were sent to bed. And then Kular told us what had happened to him.

It began, he said, with cotton.

# 9

There was, Kular said, a great land called Tarn, which stretched north to the snows and south to the desert, east to the mountains and west to the ocean. It was bigger than any of us could imagine, the biggest nation in the world.

We all nodded: we had heard of Tarn from Mizan the Trader. Tarn had once been ruled by a cruel king and his nobles, and all the people were slaves, bought and sold and beaten like livestock. But many years ago there was a great uprising, and the slaves killed the king and his family. After a long war, a soldier called Tariik from the mountains became the new leader, and he decided to rebuild the land, so everyone would be free of the shackles of the old ways. There would be no more nobles, and everyone would have enough to eat.

Mizan had told us that Tariik turned out to be as cruel as the old king, and had made the land of Tarn a giant prison where children were forced to work in the mines or factories or to serve in the enormous army. And it wasn't true that everyone had enough to eat: there had been dreadful famines, because the soldiers came and took the food away from the farmers, and they died, and then there was no one left to work the land. But even so, many people still thought it was better than being a slave of the nobles. Which showed, said Mizan, how bad the nobles had been.

Tariik was long dead, but Mizan had said that Tarn was still the same. "Now there are new bosses, same as the old bosses," he had said. "Whoever is in charge, they are always rich." We remembered Mizan's words when Kular told us about Tarn. Mizan's stories had made it seem a strange and frightening place, but we didn't think it had anything to do with us. Kular's story made us realize that Tarn wasn't so far away, after all.

Kular said that a few days' journey upriver, the River ran through the southern reaches of Tarn. That was arid country, inhabited only by a few villages and herds of small deer and desert foxes. One day, the boss of a big company looked at a map, and he saw the empty spaces of the Upper Pembar Plains and the blue line of the River running through them. And he put his fat forefinger on the map, and said, "We will grow cotton here. There is water. There is space."

So the company had sent engineers and agriculturalists and workers south to the Pembar, hundreds of them in wagons and trucks, and they built settlements along the River and began to dig a series of canals to irrigate the fields. The workers were white-skinned and spoke a strange tongue, and they were dressed in shabby clothes that didn't keep them warm. The men in charge wore polished boots and clean grey uniforms, and they carried guns and whips. The locals thought the workers must be prisoners from Tarn.

At first the Pembar people took no notice of the foreigners, since they settled at a distance from the villages. Some even said it might be a good thing, bringing money and trade; but those with foresight prophesied trouble.

The first sign, as always, was the River. The earthworks muddied the drinking water, but that wasn't the worst of it. Downriver from the cotton fields, animals and crops began to die of mysterious sicknesses that no one could explain. The villagers said the water was poisoned by the chemicals the company used to keep the cotton free of pests. Some villagers rowed upstream to the new settlements and saw the irrigation works with their own eyes. They returned pale with shock: they said that the cotton fields stretched as far as the eye could see, that the earth was scarred with gigantic piles of upthrown yellow earth and that the workers were as numerous as ants. They understood then that the Tarnish were planning to steal their river to feed the cotton. "Cotton is thirsty," said Kular. "It needs a lot of water."

When the angry villagers demanded to be paid for their losses, the chief engineer told them to go away, and when they wouldn't leave, he called up the soldiers, who fired their guns over their heads and set fierce dogs on them. After that, the villagers were afraid, but they were also angry.

The wars didn't start until the level of the River began to fall. Kular was unsure what had happened next, because there were many different stories. The villagers began to attack the irrigation works, creeping upstream at night to wreak acts of sabotage: a lock broken here, an engine destroyed there. Every time something was broken, the Tarnish took their revenge on the Pembar people. Soldiers would come to a village and arrest young men at random, forcing them to work on the canals with the Tarnish prisoners. That was a harsh sentence, because the Tarnish hated the Pembar people. The Tarnish prisoners stole their food and beat them, and if the young men tried to escape, they were often caught and shot. When they died, their bodies were thrown without ceremony into the River, to be found by their grieving families or to rot, undiscovered and unshriven, far away from home.

The hatred between the Pembar and the Tarnish people grew thick and bloody until at last, in the middle of the previous winter, the chief engineer was murdered. Some said his throat had been cut, others said that he had been shot, some said it was villagers who did it, others that it was his own workers. Whatever happened, the Tarnish men blamed the Pembar people. The army ordered that an entire village a few miles north of Kular's be burned down, and every grown man shot dead. So that is what the soldiers did. And the workers kept building the canals and farming the cotton just as if nothing had happened.

"After that," said Kular, "it was open war." He paused and looked down at the table, his face dark with grief and hatred. "We cannot win," he said. "They have machine guns and soldiers, and we have a few rifles, a few angry farmers." For a moment his eyes went blank again. "They shot my wife," he said. "They came to our village and burned it down, and they murdered women and children. And they shot my wife as we were fleeing in the boat. They don't care what they do. Yet we have no choice but to fight them. If we have no water, we cannot live."

We all nodded. This is something River folk understand in their bones. Now we knew why our River had sunk so low this summer.

"But it's not so bad here," said my father uncertainly. "Even though there is a drought. We're a long way from the cotton fields."

A strange expression crossed Kular's face. "That was what our village said last spring," he said. "Do you think they will stop? They are still building the irrigation works. There are already fields of cotton as far as you can see, but they want more. They say they will make the Plains of Pembar look like a snowfield. Every year they will plant more cotton, and every year there will be less water for us. They don't care if we starve.

They don't care if they poison the water. And they are killing the River. Soon it will die, and so will we."

There was a silence, and I knew that all of us were afraid. I glanced at my grandmother, and I saw that none of this was news to her. She had already seen it in the Book.

"They will not stop," said Grandmother. "The only thing that will stop them will be when the River is dead and the plains have turned to desert sands. It will not take so long. But soldiers will not come to this place, even if they send famine before them."

She turned to Kular. "If you would like to stay, you and your son will be safe here. For a little while."

# 10

I read Kular's story to Mely this morning, and she asked me what it had to do with anything. "You didn't leave the village because of the River," she said. "You left because of the Book. That's what you told me, anyway."

It annoyed me, because it was Mely who had said that it was my story to tell how I thought best. And in any case, I told her, what happened to the River is part of what happened to the Book. They are the same thing.

"It's stupidity," said Mely darkly. "That is how they are the same. Human beings are selfish and greedy and they think that the world has been put there just for them."

Mely is always saying that people are stupid. "I'm a human being too," I said.

"I didn't say *all* human beings," said Mely. Before I could answer, she stuck her tail up and went outside to lie in the sun, and that was the end of that. I sighed and sat down at my table in my tiny kitchen, and I looked out of the window at the old fig tree that grows outside. It has dark glossy leaves and beautiful grey branches that are softly curved, like a woman's arms, and it is always full of birds that squabble and court in its deep shade. The fig tree was the reason why I rented this flat, and looking at it always makes me feel better.

We live in the Old Quarter, in the middle of a tangle of alleyways that are always strung with washing. When it rains, the alleys flood and the whole quarter stinks of sewage, and so I am glad we live on the first floor, where we escape most of the mud. Many of the buildings were once grand houses, with wide courtyards and graceful windows covered in iron grilles and carved wooden shutters, but they have long since lost their grandeur: the bright paint has faded on the shutters, and the stucco has fallen off the bricks, and their gardens are gone wild with tangles of brambles and prickly pear. They have been divided up into rooming houses or small flats, like the one I live in.

The Old Quarter has a bad reputation. Several notorious gangs are based here, and every now and then a war breaks out that makes big headlines in the newspaper. When that happens, locals stay away from known gang territories like the fish market, and they never linger in the streets. Although the gangs are mainly interested in shooting each other, it is always possible for someone to get in the way of a bullet accidentally. I suppose it is the same wherever you live. River folk never go swimming where there are currents that pull you down, and they know that you don't take the boat out in storms, and that you stay away from water snakes.

There are two gangsters who keep an eye on my street. They are young men with sharp haircuts and expensive leather jackets, and they stand on the corner smoking expensive foreign cigarettes. I have lived here long enough for the men to nod when I walk past, and I nod back. The strange thing is that I don't feel threatened by them. Perhaps I ought to be afraid, but I am not important enough to interest them. The truth is that

I feel much less safe near the Financial District, where the businessmen go to the nightclubs and stagger out with crooked ties and bloodshot eyes and leer at me as I hurry home from a late appointment.

I never see my customers at home. I hire a stall in the tourist market four days a week. Sometimes people ask me where I live, and when I tell them they open their eyes wide and tell me I must be very brave to live in such a dangerous area by myself. Sometimes they ask if they can visit me, because they think it will be an adventure, but I always refuse. My home is private.

Anyway, I sat on my chair and stared at the fig tree and thought about what Mely had said. She is right: I haven't spoken much about the Book, although it was the reason I left the village. I suspect that's because it hurts to think about it. Sometimes, when I feel lost or I don't know what to do, I still think to myself that I must ask the Book, momentarily forgetting that it has gone. And then I remember with a jolt, and I feel that terrible emptiness all over again.

11

To question the Book was very simple. You just took it out of the box and laid it on the table, and held the question in your mind as you opened it. There was no ritual or ceremony, but it was important to be respectful, both to the question and to the Book, and to have a clear and open mind. Some questions were more significant than others, and with those ones – we always knew if they were big questions – we would prepare ourselves with meditation and fasting. But questions of that kind were rare.

You knew the answer at once when you saw it. Sometimes it was on the first page you opened, but sometimes you had to leaf through page after page before you found it. It's hard to describe how you knew: it was as if the words shone out of the page, although they never actually looked any different from the words around them. And when you found the answer, there was no guarantee that anyone would understand it, at least at first. Most often the answer became clear in time, but sometimes it didn't. Sometimes, my grandmother used to say, people just ask the wrong question.

Whenever I opened the Book, whether for a question or just to read it, I felt a faint tingle in the tips of my fingers. And no matter how many times I did it, I felt a flutter of excitement in my stomach. The Book always had the same black and red lettering and the same thick, fragrant paper, but the words were always different. I don't know how often I read it through from cover and cover and then returned to the beginning, to start again with an entirely different Book.

Inside the Book, as my grandmother often told me, was written everything that had been, everything that was and everything that was to come. And all these things changed all the time.

When I looked into the Book for my own interest and pleasure, it usually told me stories. I found in the Book some of the stories that Grandmother told us, and I knew that she had discovered them here too. When my duties were done, I would spend hours in the room with the Book, devouring its endless treasury. Some stories were funny, some were tragic, some were frightening and some I didn't understand at all; but I thought all of them were beautiful.

The Book didn't only contain stories. My mother most often found poems. Grandmother usually got recipes (some very good ones, she said). There could be instructions on how to build a cupboard or how to gut a fish, or a table of the phases of the moon, or the names of the major constellations in five different languages, or there could be lists of the properties of precious stones or herbs or sacred trees, or a description of the habits of animals I had never heard of, or a history of a realm that had fallen a thousand years ago in a land thousands of miles away, or a lexicon of a forgotten language.

Sometimes, although not very often, there were pictures – intricate drawings like the one I saw the first time I looked at the Book with my mother. Grandmother told me that once she had opened the Book to find that every page was blank, but that had never happened to me. I often wondered what question the Book refused to answer, but of course, she couldn't say.

The day after Kular told us about the cotton fields, I asked the Book a serious question. I was afraid in a way I hadn't been before. There had always been things to fear – accident, famine, drought, disease – but they were part of the texture of life as I knew it. The things Kular spoke of came from a world I didn't understand. I remembered my grandmother's face after she had asked the Book her own questions. I didn't dare ask her what she had read there. Since my mother had died, Grandmother seemed shrunken. She was still kindly most of the time, and she did her duties as the head woman of the house, but for the first time I understood that she was old.

I fasted all day and then, in the middle of the afternoon when the house was quiet, I washed myself and oiled my hair and braided it, and I went into the room and took the Book out of its box and placed it with special care on the table. I stared at it for a long time before I opened it. I took a deep breath and asked my question: What did the Tarnish cotton fields bode for us? And then I opened the Book.

The answer was only one word. It was all alone on the page, in red letters that seemed to blaze out of the paper.

*Change.*

# 12

Despite the Book's message, life continued much the same for the next year or so. We watched the River anxiously all through the winter; the banks were now ridged with lines that showed the lowering water levels over the years, and still it sank lower and lower, finger by finger, handspan by handspan. It was a big river, deep and strong, but that winter we felt its life faltering. When spring came it rose a few feet, and our hearts lightened; but by midsummer it had shrunk again, until it reached its lowest mark ever.

My sister Shiha married in the spring, a handsome man called Indra from the next village downriver. The wedding went on for three days, with feasting and music and dancing. Shiha was a year younger than I was, but, unlike me, she was impatient to get married. She was like a bright fruit ripening in the sun, warm and luscious. She took after my mother, and I took after my father; like him, I was thin and dark, and my hair was straight and dull, where hers fell in glossy ringlets about her face. Although no one looked at me if Shiha was anywhere

47

near by, it never occurred to me to envy her. I loved to watch her when her face was in repose: as she spun wool, or made the spelt cakes that were her speciality, or plucked a sweet melody from her *tar*. She was always my favourite sister. Before she climbed into the garlanded boat with her new husband, she embraced me, laughing and crying at the same time.

"Oh, Sim, I am so happy," she said. "But I am so sad, too! I will miss you so much!"

I kissed her glowing cheek and told her not to be silly. I was truly happy for her: their marriage was a love match, and Indra came from a kind family who I knew would be good to her. But my steps home that evening felt heavy, and when we sat down for a light meal of leftovers – none of us were hungry after the heavy feasting of the wedding – I felt that our house was like the River, more shrunken every day.

After the wedding, Kular moved out of our house, where he had stayed through the winter. He was a courteous guest, a gentle and shy man who rendered his thanks by working for my father. He remained in the village, moving in with old Tankar, who needed the help in his fields, and who lived alone, very close to Sulihar, who was still caring for Kular's little boy.

Kular was only the first of those fleeing the Upper Pembar cotton fields; refugees became a common sight in our village. We saw whole families floating downriver on laden boats. Sometimes they stopped and bought food from us or, more rarely, begged it; but they never stayed. They told us their stories and moved on, heading to the cities in the east, where they might find a way to make a living.

A month or so after the wedding, Mizan made his annual visit, bearing goods and news. His boat chugged to our landing and all the village children came running and cheering, followed more sedately by the rest of the village. The children wore their embroidered holiday clothes, because Mizan's visits were always an occasion for a festival. The river was so low that he struggled to clamber onto the pier, puffing and spluttering, and he bent over to regain his breath before he handed out his annual offering of sweets and nuts to the children.

His assistant, Taret, a skinny, dark-bearded man with one eye, swung up easily after him and grinned at the crowd. And then everyone went quiet, because a stranger followed them onto the pier. She was a tall, white-skinned woman with dark red hair tied back from her face. At first we thought she was Tarnish. She was dressed in jeans and a T-shirt and sunglasses, and a small, silver box was slung around her neck on a black strap. She looked clean and sharp, like a steel blade, and I felt uncomfortable because I couldn't see her eyes behind the black discs that covered them. I suddenly felt quaint and childish in my silk embroidered dress.

It turned out that she wasn't Tarnish at all. She came from a country further away than Tarn, Mizan said, a country that lay across a wide sea, and her name was Jane Watson. She was writing a book about the people who lived on the River, and she wanted to meet us and talk to us about our lives.

At the mention of a book, the villagers turned to look at her with respect. We all thought she must be some kind of Keeper. I studied her with fascination. I had never seen a woman like Jane Watson before. She stood on the pier, her feet far apart, unworried by the fact that the whole village was staring at her in silence. She greeted us in our own language, with an accent none of us had heard before, and smiled. My father courteously returned her greeting, and then Mizan and Taret began to haul their wares out of the boat and set up their stall on the bank beside the pier, and we all got on with our trading.

Jane Watson stood a little apart, out of the way, and took photographs. I knew what a camera was – Lukman, one of my cousins, had an old black camera which was one of his most precious possessions, although he could never use it because he didn't have any film, or any way of developing the photographs even if he found some. And a few of us had made the journey downriver to Kilok, where for a small sum a photographer would take portraits that were then displayed proudly on the walls back home. But I'd never seen one as small and shiny as Jane Watson's. I only knew what it was because I asked Mizan.

"She takes pictures," he said, shrugging. "All the time. I think she's crazy. But she's paying me well, so she can do what she likes."

"Is she a Keeper?" I asked.

Mizan glanced quickly up at me. "I don't think they have Keepers where she comes from," he said.

I was burning with curiosity, but I knew now was not the time for idle chatter. There was a long line behind me, and much business to be done. I sold Mizan my lengths of cloth for a good price, and bought salt and oil for the house and a pair of pretty enamel earrings for myself, sealing the deal with a hand-clasp. Then I left. Jane Watson was still taking photographs, surrounded by a gaggle of curious children who were keeping a respectful distance. I glanced over at her, and she looked up. Although I couldn't see her eyes, I knew she was watching me. Then she swung the camera up to her face, and I felt a sudden strange horror at its blank gaze. I turned away and hurried off, clutching my purchases to my breast.

# 13

When I think of Jane Watson now, I don't feel angry. It seems strange: not so long ago, I hated her with a passion that frightened me. A wild animal crouched in my chest, and it seemed it would take the smallest gesture for that animal to leap out and tear everything to pieces, rending flesh, tearing skin, breaking bones. And I would have been glad to let it go, I would have set that savage beast at Jane Watson's throat and I would have been happy to see her scream in agony, I would have rejoiced to see her blood spill steaming onto the ground.

And yet, despite my initial distrust, despite what happened afterwards, the truth is that for a while I liked Jane Watson. While Mizan went upriver to do his trading, she stayed in our village for almost a month, taking photographs so constantly that we ceased to notice it. She lived among us, learning the pattern of our days. She helped to feed the pigs and the sheep, and learned how to open and close the locks on our irrigation channels, and hoed our crops and lit incense at the temple. She taught me some of her language, which meant that later, when I came to the city, I could talk to the tourists and make my living. Each night she sat down with us and ate our bread and salt.

When Mizan returned, we held a farewell feast. We sang her our most beautiful songs, and she told us how grateful she was for our generosity and our trust. I cried because she was going away, because I would miss her. She had told me so many interesting things about the places she had visited and the country where she had been born. And she kissed me on both cheeks, and said that one day we would see each other again.

She went to sleep in the bed that I had made for her, and rose with the sun. She washed her face and broke her fast and then we all went down to the River to wave her goodbye. Stepping onto Mizan's boat, she turned to face us, the pale early sun shining behind her head so she seemed to be wearing a halo of copper. She held her hand high in the air until she vanished around the next bend.

Later that day, several hours after she had left, we discovered that some time between nightfall and sunrise Jane Watson had slipped secretly into the room where we kept the Book. She had taken the Book out of its old box, which only the Keepers were ever allowed to do, and had hidden it in her bag, and when she left with Mizan, the Book left with her.

Jane Watson stole the Book. And after that, nothing was ever the same again.

14

My memories of the days after the Book was stolen are all in fragments. I remember my grandmother's pale face, her eyes bright with unshed tears, and my father's mouth, set in a stern, hard line. I remember that a storm blew in from the mountains, and I watched the nut trees thrashing against the luminous yellow sky and the leaves flying off into the darkening night. I remember the endless visitors from the village, a stream of them for days. Everyone wanted to see the empty box, the violated room, everyone wanted to touch the Keeper's shoulder, as one touches the shoulder of a mourner.

When they heard what had happened, the brothers Yani and Sopli took their motorboat and headed downriver in pursuit of Mizan. "We'll get the Book back, don't you worry!" they said to me, grinning, their dark eyes flashing at the challenge. "We have the fastest boat on the river!" And they spat into the brown waves and chugged off, their wake furling behind them in white wings, and my heart rose.

They returned three days later, their hands empty, their

faces downcast. They had caught up with Mizan at Kilok, a day downriver, and he had been horrified when he heard what had happened. But Jane Watson, perhaps knowing that she would be pursued, had already left Mizan's boat. She had met an associate, a bald man with golden spectacles who drove a jeep, and they had gone south over the plains, away from the River.

"I didn't know," Mizan told Yani and Sopli. "By the gods, if I had known, I would have beaten that woman within an inch of her life! I would have got it back for you! I am ashamed that I brought such bad luck to your people. But I didn't know."

Yani and Sopli had no way of following a jeep overland, and so they came back home and told us what they had found out. When I saw their expressions, I felt something inside me clench like a fist. The brothers looked crushed and humiliated, as if something in their souls had shrivelled in shame at their failure to bring back the Book. But they didn't steal it, I thought, and they don't deserve to feel ashamed. Jane Watson should feel ashamed.

I wondered whether she had any human feelings, this woman who I had so foolishly trusted, to whom I had revealed some of my most secret thoughts. I imagined bitterly how she must have laughed at me as she pretended to listen sympathetically, her brows drawn in a straight line of concentration. I thought about the bald man with spectacles she had met in Kilok; it sounded as if Jane Watson had planned to meet him, as if there had been a plot. I wondered if Jane Watson had intended to steal the Book from the beginning.

At first the theft was a wound that went too deep for pain. The Book was our soul, our oracle, our delight and our pride. It was our friend. Without its guidance, who were we? Without its light, how would we see? Jane Watson's action went beyond betrayal, into the incomprehensible. We simply didn't understand why she had taken the Book. No one but the Keepers knew how to read it. In her hands it was useless; it would be just an object, inert and dead. And yet she had dared to take it from us. A great anger tore through the village. If Jane Watson had reappeared in those days, the gentle villagers I had known all my life would have torn her to pieces as if they were tigers.

Our anger was partly fear. Jane Watson had casually destroyed hundreds of years of tradition when she took the Book out of the box, just as the Tarnish soldiers were destroying villages that had stood on the River since people had first walked into the Pembar Plains. Things that once had been solid now were uncertain, the ground seemed to echo beneath our feet like a thin layer of rock over a great, measureless hollow that plunged to the centre of the earth. We saw the sun rise each morning with relief, as if we feared in our dreams that it might vanish overnight.

To the last question I ever asked, the Book had answered *Change*. I hadn't expected that the change would be the loss of the Book itself.

I thought of the first night Jane Watson had dined with us, when she had begun to win my trust. She had taken off her sunglasses as she stepped inside, holding them loosely in one hand as she greeted our family, and at last I could see her eyes. They were pale blue, large and finely formed, with long fair lashes. Her skin was freckled, her eyebrows broad and straight, and her mouth was set firmly, as if she were always in the process of making a difficult decision. Her face was dour and stubborn, but when she smiled her whole face lit up with an attractive humour. I had never seen anyone like her before.

I could see at once that Grandmother didn't trust Jane Watson. She was being very polite, and her face was expressionless and wary. It wasn't only that Jane Watson was a stranger, and a foreigner at that; it was because Grandmother knew, as I knew too once I saw Jane Watson's eyes, that she was a woman of power. It was a strange power, and heavily veiled; but it was palpable in the charge in my skin as she sat next to me at the table in one of the designated places for honoured guests.

She complimented our house and the meal, speaking haltingly, but without making many mistakes. She had learned our language well, and soon she and I were talking. She said she was very interested in the people of the Pembar. "Nothing has changed here for centuries, because the Pembar Plains are so remote," she said. "And your traditions and customs can give us some insight into things that have disappeared elsewhere."

At the mention of change, I looked up sharply. "Nowhere can escape change," I said. "Perhaps you've heard of what's happening upriver, with the Tarnish cotton fields."

She nodded. "We have heard of it," she said. "The refugees are telling terrible stories, which are being told even in my country. That's partly why I'm making this journey now. Perhaps I can help your people, by showing others what is threatened here."

"They are stealing our River," I said. "If the River dies, we cannot stay here. We won't be able to live."

"There was already a drought, was there not?" said Jane Watson. "Some things are beyond even the Tarnish. Rivers die in the normal course of nature. The world is changing; the weather is changing. Some things will vanish, no matter what we do."

Her words gave me a chill in my stomach, and speaking of the death of our River with a stranger seemed disrespectful, so I changed the subject, asking her the first thing that came into my head.

"Are you a Keeper as well?" I asked.

Jane Watson smiled, and her face transformed; she seemed

suddenly like a little girl, amused and excited. "Why do you ask?"

"I don't know. You feel like a Keeper. But Mizan said that you don't have Keepers in your country."

"We don't have the same powers that you do," said Jane Watson. "And yet, among my own people, you might say I am a kind of Keeper."

I met her clear gaze. "You are clearly a woman of power," I said.

"Like knows like," said Jane Watson, smiling again. "Yes, I can see the power in you, just as it is in me. In my homeland we have many kinds of power, but we have lost the way of some ancient arts that you have been wise enough to preserve." She suddenly looked shy. "I have heard of your Book. I should – I should like very much to see it for myself, if you would show me."

I felt a flutter of pride that our Book was so famous that a foreigner like Jane Watson had heard of it, and promised to show her the Book later.

After the food had been eaten and the table cleared, she followed me solemnly into the room off the kitchen, and watched alertly as I took it from the box and opened it.

"What would you like to ask it?" I said.

"Do I have to ask a question?" said Jane Watson.

"No," I said. "But you can if you like."

"Oh." She thought for a moment, and then said, "What would the Book like to tell me?"

"That's your question?"

She nodded. I held the question in my mind and opened the Book. Jane Watson moved close as I opened the covers, and I glanced up. Her eyes were shining, her lips slightly parted, and I noticed that her hands were trembling.

On one page was a picture, an engraving of a lonely, flat landscape wound through by a river, and a flock of cranes were flying over the horizon. On the other page was a single line of text.

"What does it say?" asked Jane Watson.

"The picture is of the Plains of Pembar," I said. "That's our River. And it's one phrase. It says: *What profit it a man if he gains the world and loses his soul?*"

For a moment Jane Watson looked astonished, and then she covered it with a laugh. "I wonder what that means," she said. Her voice was shaky, and she was slightly pale. I wondered what the words meant to her.

"I don't know," I said. "Only you can know what the words mean. And sometimes it takes a long time to find out. It doesn't often happen that the reading is alone on the page. It means that it's important, that the Book wants to make sure you hear."

I waited, hoping that Jane Watson would explain, as the phrase clearly meant something to her. It was impolite to ask directly. But she didn't. Instead she reached out with the tip of her finger and gently stroked the page. I flinched and snatched it away: it was forbidden for anyone except the Keepers to touch the Book. A curious expression briefly crossed her face, a kind of lust mixed with frustration or anger, but it passed so swiftly I almost thought I had imagined it. Jane Watson apologized for her rudeness, and I dismissed her gesture as ignorant and clumsy rather than sinister, and forgot all about it.

I remembered that expression after Jane Watson left, when I was tormenting myself with reproaches: I ought to have taken it as a warning, I ought to have been more wary. Back then, it was not my way to be suspicious. When Grandmother told me that Jane Watson had a cold soul and was not to be trusted, I defended her hotly. I said that Jane Watson could help us against the Tarns, and that we should not behave like foolish backward villagers, afraid of the new. I said things that make me blush now when I think of them.

Grandmother shook her head and said nothing more. Later she told me that Jane Watson had enchanted me, and there was nothing more to say until the spell was broken. And when the spell did break, Grandmother did not once rebuke me, not by word nor by glance. That hurt almost more than anything else. I think it was Grandmother's silence that made me decide to find Jane Watson myself, and to bring the Book back where it belonged.

15

When I think back, I can't quite believe that I made the choice to leave my village so casually. I didn't consult anyone, not even Grandmother. I just decided, and then I left. I suppose it was partly a question of pride: without the Book, I had no place in the village. I knew that my family didn't need me: there were my brothers and sisters to care for my grandmother and father as they aged. I was a Keeper of the Book, and so had my place, an important place. When the Book was stolen, I had nothing. I couldn't face my loss of status. Writing it down, I realize how vain my decision was. I suspect I didn't speak to my grandmother about it because she would have pointed out my vanity, and underneath I was slightly ashamed of it – although I don't know whether she would still have approved of my seeking the Book. But at the time I didn't think about any of this. I just decided, and then I acted.

I took the dinghy that had belonged to my mother and that had become mine when she died, and I packed it with supplies – flatbreads, smoked fish, dried fruits, a big bag of walnuts, drinking water. I filled a purse with my hoarded cache of coins, squirrelled away from my weaving, along with some small things that were precious to me – the gold earrings my grandmother had given me when I was presented at the temple, a bracelet of amber that had belonged to my mother – and tied it around my belly, where it would be safe and hidden. I had a little more money than usual, because Jane Watson's arrival had meant that I hadn't spent as much as I normally would at Mizan's stall. I packed two blankets and some spare clothes and a small, very sharp clasp knife that I kept in a sheath on my belt.

Then I wrote a note for my family, saying that I was going to find the Book, and would send word. I left one morning before first light, a week after Jane Watson. By now it was late summer, but there was as yet no sign of the chills of autumn. I unmoored the dinghy from the pier behind our house and rowed out to the centre of the River; then I shipped the oars and drifted downstream, watching the sun rise. It was a beautiful, clear summer dawn; the air brightened until it was like liquid light, and the River rippled molten gold. Somewhere very high overhead I could hear the lonely twittering of a lark, but that served only to deepen the silence that filled the world.

I realized it was the first time I had been properly alone for many days. Then I thought, with a thrill of excitement that was not unmixed with fear, that I was more alone than I had ever been in my life. I lay back in the dinghy and stared up at the sky. Even though I had just made the most momentous decision of my life, I felt deeply peaceful. I had given my destiny to the River, and for that moment all the guilt and anger and sorrow that had filled me for days melted away.

I had no clear idea what I would do. I thought I'd travel to Kilok and ask if anyone had seen Jane Watson. Yani and Sopli had come back because they couldn't travel overland, but

I thought that Jane Watson would have to come back to the River at some point, because it was still the major road in this part of the world. Beyond Kilok, I really hadn't thought much. This was partly because Kilok was as far from home as I had ever been. I didn't know what the world was like beyond it, and I didn't have the Book to ask. I missed it most fiercely in those early days, when I so needed its advice.

I made one sensible decision: to dress as a boy. Jane Watson had told me that it could be dangerous for women to travel alone. She kept a gun, which she wore on a shoulder holster hidden beneath her jacket when she was travelling. She showed it to me once: it was quite small, a revolver, which she said was standard issue for city traffic police, and which she had bought on the black market when she had arrived in our country. I weighed it in my hand briefly before giving it back to her with a shudder; it was surprisingly heavy and the metal felt cold and deadly. I had no idea how to fire a gun, and had never thought to learn. Now I wished I had taken the trouble. It wouldn't have been so hard; Sopli had a gun and would have taught me, if I had asked him. But now it was too late, and all I had to protect me was my knife.

On the other hand, it would take a sharp eye to pick me as a girl. As I floated downriver, I cut my braid off at the nape of my neck with my clasp knife. Although the blade was sharp, it took a while to saw through my thick hair, and when I had finished I held the severed plait in my hands for some time, breathing heavily, before I threw it in the water. The air felt cold on the back of my neck. The plaited hair twirled on the ripples for a while and then drifted off to the bank, where it snagged on some reeds. I watched its fate with a curious mixture of sadness and liberation. It was as if, with that gesture, I had thrown away my childhood.

Now my hair was short, it would be easier to look after, and no one would think I was a girl. I have always been skinny, and my small breasts were easily hidden in a baggy shirt. With my worn sandals, shin-length trousers and sun-bleached shirt, I looked exactly like a water rat, one of the ragged orphan boys who hustle a living up and down the water, making deliveries, running errands, catching fish or freshwater crabs.

I let the current take me for the rest of the day, only exerting myself to ensure that I didn't ground on any shoals. I listened to the many voices of the River and watched the banks drift by, raising my hand occasionally when I passed farmers hoeing their fields or cleaning out the irrigation channels on the banks. I didn't think about my family, who by now would have discovered my letter. I didn't want to think about them, because it would hurt: they would be bewildered, grieving, worried; they might even be angry with me. I didn't think about the Book, or where I was going. I just lay back in my boat and squinted up at the sky and let myself be empty. For the first time in my life, I was no one: I had left behind everything that I knew and everyone who knew me. I didn't feel sad or lost or confused, or anything that I might have expected. I think what I felt more than anything else was relief.

# 16

When I read Mely the last chapter this morning, she stood up and stretched from her nose to the tip of her tail. Then she yawned delicately, showing every one of her white, sharp teeth. Finally, after all that pantomime, she deigned to tell me what she thought.

"That," Mely said, "is a pack of lies."

I should be used to Mely by now, but this offended me.

"Lies?" I said. "I am trying to be as truthful as I possibly can. And how can you know, anyway? I haven't met you yet. You weren't even there."

"I met you very soon after that," said Mely. "And you didn't seem at all relieved to me. You were lost and confused and sad, all the things that you say you weren't."

I sighed. "That was *afterwards*," I said. "I felt all those things *afterwards*. Not on the first day…"

"That's why I felt sorry for you," said Mely. "Because you were so lost."

"You felt sorry for me? As I remember, it was *me* who took

64

pity on *you*. *You* were the one without anywhere to live and with no food…"

Mely scratched her ear, pretending that she hadn't heard me. She doesn't like to be reminded about that.

"And," I added, "I'm still the one who buys the fish heads. So it might be a good idea to be polite to me."

"You said you wanted me to be honest," said Mely. "And look what happens when I tell you what I think! You threaten to starve me!"

"You can be honest without being rude," I said.

"I told you a cat doesn't know anything about storytelling. So why do you ask me? It's your fault if you get offended."

"You like listening to Blind Harim as much as I do," I said. "So you must know something about telling stories."

"Anyway, you might tell lies about me," said Mely, who wasn't listening. "I'm not a story, I'm your friend. What if you say things that aren't true? Won't you be changing how things are?"

So now I understand that Mely is worried about this book, because she is part of the story. When I think about it, she's right. Books *do* change things. My Book changed things all the time: people took its advice and lived better lives (or didn't take its advice, and lived worse lives; but they knew what they should have done). It's hard to see how this book I'm writing will change things, really; it's a different sort of book, for a start. But I can see why Mely might not want to be a story cat in a story book.

In the end, I promised to be as truthful as I possibly could, especially when I wrote about Mely, because being truthful would change things the least. Mely looked suspicious, but thought that would probably be all right. There are two problems with this: the first is that I suspect that being truthful changes things more than lying does. The Book was powerful, my grandmother told me, because it was always truthful; there might be another kind of power in distorting reality with words, but it will always prove weaker than truthfulness.

On the other hand, Grandmother also said that truthfulness has many faces, and that some of those faces might look like lies. "You can never be quite certain," she said. "And that is a good thing, because only a god can be certain about the truth, and even then only sometimes. It is much harder to be a human being than it is to be a god."

Aside from questions about the gods, the other problem is that I don't think Mely will like it much if I do tell the truth, because it doesn't always show her in a good light. Although she'd never admit it, I think that she wouldn't mind if I wrote down a pack of lies about her, as long as they were flattering. Fond as I am of her (and I am very fond of Mely – that is the truth too), she is sometimes very annoying.

As Mely said, we met in Kilok, two days after I left my village, and by then I no longer felt at all peaceful. I was lost and confused and sad.

I know now that Kilok is a small town, but it is much bigger than my village, which is little more than a single road lined with houses and fields and orchards. I had been there many times with my father, who often brought cheese and fish to sell at the market, but never on my own. To me, Kilok seemed bewildering and enormous. I came ashore upstream, just where the houses began, and dragged my boat up onto the bank and covered it with brush to hide it from unfriendly eyes. Then I walked through the straggly outskirts into the market square, my shadow stretching long behind me in the rich light of evening.

I had unthinkingly expected the market to be bustling, as it had been every time I had seen it, but of course by then everyone had finished their business for the day and gone home.

A couple of stray dogs nosed about for scraps, and an old man squatted by the well clutching his walking stick and staring blindly into space, but otherwise it was deserted.

The mood of peaceful certainty that had accompanied me down the River all day evaporated like spit on a hot griddle. It dawned on me for the first time that I had no idea what I was doing. What had I been thinking? What was I going to do now?

I stood in the middle of the empty marketplace as the dusk deepened. A noisy bunch of starlings was squabbling in a locust tree and, further off, I could hear the faint shouts of children playing and the plaintive bleats of goats being brought in for the evening's milking. A couple of people walked through the square and stared at me incuriously as they passed. I saw myself suddenly as others did: a scruffy, skinny lad. Even the dogs took absolutely no notice of me.

I almost turned around and went home. It would be a couple of days' hard row upriver, and inside I flinched at the thought. Then I remembered the shame in Yani and Sopli's eyes when they had returned empty-handed from Kilok. I felt that shame already burning in my stomach, and I knew now it was shame at my own powerlessness. I couldn't turn back yet. My pride wouldn't let me.

At the same time, I didn't have the first clue what to do next. The thought of knocking on one of those doorways, of facing the sceptical eyes of a stranger, made my heart shrivel. As I stood there, caught between one action and another, the sun set and a fat orange moon rose, throwing strange shadows everywhere. In its unwavering light the houses looked sinister and dangerous, and I shivered as I made my way back to my boat. At first I missed it, I had hidden it too well, and for a few horrible moments I thought someone had stolen it. But then, with a rush of relief, I put my hands on its friendly wood, and I scrambled into its bows as if I were coming home. Which was true, really; that boat was now all I had of home.

I pulled out my blankets and made myself a bed of springy branches nestled inside the sheltering hull of my boat. The night was mild and clear, and I lay on my back looking up with burning, sleepless eyes through the shrubby branches at the stars burning in the luminous dark blue sky. I had been sitting idly in the boat all day, so I wasn't tired, and now my thoughts chased each other around and around in my head like a lot of stupid, frightened puppies.

Mainly my thoughts were telling me I had just made the most foolish decision of my life.

# 17

I didn't sleep at all that night. I lay back and watched the white ship of the moon on her long voyage above me. As the hours passed I felt my soul sinking, as if I were floating down through darkness, as if I were falling away from the moon and the world silvered by her light into an endless, black ocean. The waters beneath me were still and deep, and as each hour passed I sank more deeply into the darkness, further from the light, into a world that was ever more silent and more heavy.

I think I hadn't really believed until that night in Kilok that the Book was gone. I had somehow kept the knowledge from myself. Now I couldn't escape it.

There aren't proper words for pain. When you hurt your body, or when you suffer toothache or a bad headache, the pain fills the whole world, and the only way to express it is to scream or groan; and then, when it's over, you don't remember it. The pain vanishes and your body forgets. I suppose it's because if your body remembered what pain was like, it would be frightened all the time. It's the same with grief or loneliness. Nobody can really know what pain is like for another person. Words can point towards the feeling, but they can't describe it. You just have to hope that the person to whom you're trying to describe the experience has felt similar pain themselves, because then they might nod and say, yes. Yes, it was like that.

But even though I would like to be understood, I hope no one who reads these words has felt like I did that night in Kilok. I had felt rage and intolerable sorrow when my mother died, but at least I was in my home, with my people. In Kilok, nothing made sense any more. I had not only lost my home; I had lost its meaning. I had lost the rooftree that held my world together, the height and the depth of it, the hearth that warmed it. When I lost the Book, I lost my people and my place and the meaning of my name. I lost the picture that lived in its pages somewhere of my mother showing me its mysteries for the first time, and I lost the voice that led me through my doubts and fears and showed me the path forward. I lost my past and my future. I lost everything that told me who I was. And I lost my place in the village. If I was not the Keeper, then who was I?

That night was the first time I tasted despair. But in the chill hours before dawn, I found that the ocean was not bottomless: there was a floor, a hard ground at last, where I stopped sinking. My soul looked around and found itself in a place of irredeemable bleakness: all was colourless, flat, devoid of hope. At that moment, I was sure that I would never again feel joy. At the same time, as I stared at that grey, shadowless world, I felt as if I were made of rock, as if nothing in me could be hurt again. A great stillness began to fill me. It wasn't peacefulness exactly; it was simply that my soul had sunk as deep as it could go. The worst had happened, and I was still here. If I had not found that ground, I know I would have gone mad. Even in our village, I had seen people in great distress lose their minds. For some reason, I knew then that

I would not go mad. I'm not sure what the difference is between those who collapse into madness and those who do not, and I don't know whether it's a curse or a blessing to remain sane. Perhaps there are darker miseries that would drive my soul through the stony ground it found that night. But I suspect that even if I stumbled into worse despairs, I would still be forced to suffer them in sanity.

Gradually, as the first glimmerings of dawn began to lighten the world, I felt my body come back to life. I realized that I was cold to the marrow of my bones. I hunched the dew-damp blankets around my shoulders and shivered, waiting for the sun to rise. I felt utterly empty, as if everything that was me had been poured out and there was nothing left inside.

I slapped my legs and arms, trying to get the blood moving in them, and then, realizing I was hungry, took some flatbread and bean paste out of my bag. I was nibbling my breakfast in the bows of the boat when I heard footsteps coming my way, walking carelessly so that twigs snapped loudly and leaves crunched. I didn't feel frightened so much as shy, and I hid in the boat, hoping that whoever it was wouldn't notice me in the brush; they had probably come down for their morning's wash, and no doubt would welcome intrusion as little as I did. I peered through the branches and saw it was a stout boy about my age who, as I expected, was making his way to the edge of the river.

To my annoyance he seemed to be in no hurry to leave, and lingered by the riverbank. I bit my lip and crouched in my boat, burning with impatience; I had my own needs to attend to, after all, and it would be polite for this person to go elsewhere. I listened hard: I could hear the constant voice of the water and a couple of ducks squabbling under the shadow of the bank. There was a faint shimmer where the river cast up a pearly light that threw no illumination onto the banks. After a while,

I began to feel angry; it didn't occur to me that I was in fact the intruder, not this inconvenient but innocent stranger. I suppose I felt too tired and sad to be fair.

The light deepened and the world slowly filled up with colour, and still the figure sat unmoving on the bank. The sun edged over the horizon, sending its first level rays to dance in ripples on the river's blinding surface. I blinked, dazzled, and decided that I would clamber out of my boat and walk around noisily to announce my presence; but I stopped, spellbound, when the boy began to sing.

He had the most beautiful voice I had ever heard from a human being. It was how I imagined the gods sang, surrounded by their avatars, on the clouds that embrace Yntara, the mountain of the gods. He sang of the love-sick minstrel, the song my mother had loved and that my sister played on the *tar*, raising her sweet, husky voice. I suddenly missed them both with a savageness that I could hardly bear. In the boy's mouth the simple old melody was purer and more anguished than I had ever heard it: his voice throbbed with a liquid longing, and the song I knew so well seemed now iridescent with hues of feeling that shone through those words in ways I did not expect. I thought I had never properly heard it before; it seemed to enter my soul, and my bruised heart split open with exquisite pain.

*Let my love embrace you,*
*Your black eyes and eyebrows, Jira.*
*I burn with longing for you,*
*Cure me of this fever, Jira.*
*Let the partridge cackle*
*Like old women, Jira.*
*They cannot see into my heart.*
*Only you can see me, Jira.*

As his voice ebbed to silence on the fresh morning air, I came out of my trance and found that my cheeks were wet with tears. All my resentment at his presence had vanished. I almost walked down the bank to thank him, but I didn't want to embarrass him. He had believed he was alone, that he was pouring out this beauty in solitude, and I thought that I might startle and embarrass him.

He stayed for a few more minutes, then sighed heavily and stood up and wandered off. I followed him with my eyes until he disappeared through the scrub. The sun was now wholly risen, lifted from the horizon; I was sure he had been welcoming the new day. The boy's singing seemed a sign, a gift to show me that despair was not the sum of the world's lessons. No more panic, I told myself sternly, no more despair. I was not a child any more.

I finished my breakfast and decided that I would go into the marketplace and ask around for news of Jane Watson. If there was none, I would get back in the boat and head downstream to the next town, and I would ask there, and so on from village to village, until I heard news. There was no other way back to her country except down the River, because to the north were only the endless plains of the Tarnish empire and to the south was only desert. She would have to come back to the River; and if she did, I would hear of her.

18

"But you still haven't met *me*," said Mely pettishly this morning.

"Not yet," I said. "But you know it isn't far away."

The truth is that the thought of writing about our meeting makes me feel nervous. If I get the smallest detail incorrect, Mely will let me know in no uncertain terms. If I offend her, she will take her revenge, perhaps by sharpening her claws on my special chair, which she has promised to leave untouched, but which, all the same, I sometimes see her eyeing speculatively as she flexes her paws.

We have a pleasant routine now. If I am at home in the evening, I write in my book; and then, after breakfast in our tiny kitchen, I read what I wrote to Mely. She curls up in her chair, nose to tail, and listens hard. She is, in fact, a very good listener. It is the most peaceful part of my day. When there isn't anything to read, we still sit in the kitchen and talk, or play music on the old gramophone.

It is summer and the window is always open, so you can see the parrots and finches flashing in and out of the fig tree.

I bought some white lilies at the market yesterday and put them in a jar on the sill, and their rich scent fills the kitchen, competing with the sweet smell of ripening figs that drifts in through the window.

I didn't write anything last night, because I went out to the Stray Dog Café in the Magicians' Quarter. I go there about once a week. Mely sometimes comes with me, riding on my shoulder like an emperor riding on an elephant, but she gets bored if she is not the centre of attention, and so more often I go on my own.

I am told – usually by people who have never been there – that it is best to avoid the Magicians' Quarter. Like the Old Quarter, it has a bad reputation. It's true that it feels sinister. It's very easy to get lost if you don't pay attention, and sometimes you wonder if the streets are playing tricks on you. I first went there, in fact, to consult a magician myself, but to my disappointment he was a charlatan. Worse, he saw that I knew he was a fraud – he had enough of the powers to see that I have something of the art – and without quite threatening me openly, he made me afraid. I never went back there until my friend Yuri dragged me to the Stray Dog one bleak night last winter, when the whole world was sitting on my shoulders and weighing me down and I was as sad as sad. He said it would cheer me up, and it did.

I had never been in a place like the Stray Dog before. The only thing that signals it from the street is a crudely painted picture of a dog on the brickwork next to a sinister-looking door. Inside the door, a flight of badly lit stairs leads down into the darkness, where you find a huge man whose name is Andre. His thigh muscles are about as big as my waist, and a tall black hat makes him look even bigger, so it seems a wonder that he can fit in the narrow corridor where he sits on a stool by a shabby table, playing cards and drinking whisky. He can seem frightening until you get to know him and realize he is one of the gentlest men you are ever likely to meet. He comes from a distant country, like Jane Watson, although he told me his home is a long way away from hers, and that he comes from a northern land covered in ice. He stands out because he has white-blond hair and fair, freckled skin. He's the one who decides whether or not you can come in, and he sorts out any trouble. He won't let in anyone who looks like a secret policeman, or a thug looking for trouble, and he has an unerring instinct. Mazita, the owner of the Stray Dog, tells me that without Andre the café would have been forced to close a long time ago.

Inside, the walls are painted with strange scenes in bright colours: there are dogs in funny hats and dancing cats and horses with large, strange flowers nodding between their ears. The café is crammed with round tables with spindly legs, each with its litter of wooden chairs, none of which match, and on each table burns a fat red candle. The Stray Dog makes very good coffee and sells bad but cheap wine that gives you a fearsome headache if you drink too much of it. Mazita is an excellent cook and serves delicious little dishes of salted squid or fried bean curd or spiced vegetables. But that's not the major attraction. The reason people go is because it has the best parties in town.

There is a tiny stage against the wall backed by a sparkly silver curtain. Yuri plays there once a week. He is one of many musicians and singers who perform there, and through him I met Icana and Anna and Ling Ti. They have become friends of mine. Icana and Anna are always together, and they make a striking pair. Icana is a singer with a voice like musk and honey. She is taller than most men, and she wears long dresses of black lace and trailing embroidered shawls that show off her white skin and the startling ash-blonde hair that falls down her back. Anna is as short and brown-skinned as I am, and has black hair cropped close around her head. Her eyes are so dark they look black, and she has straight fierce eyebrows and a mouth like the bud of a rose. She has beautiful large breasts and a tiny waist, and she wears skirts and shirts with wide red belts to show off her figure. Ling Ti is tall and his hair sweeps back from his forehead. He is charming and funny and vain, and, like Anna, he is a very fine poet. It was Ling Ti who recited to me the whole of the poem that begins: *Watch for the cranes, who will bring my love to you, even as far as the Plains of Pembar…*

With Yuri and Mely, they are my closest friends in the city. They take my hand and draw me out onto the dancefloor of the Stray Dog and I find I am dancing with my heart as light as a petal tossed on a spring breeze. I laugh and meet their eyes, and they are smiling: they are happy in the music, and happy for me, and there is nothing but this moment, and this moment is all spark and dazzle, the whirl of lace and the smell of fresh sweat and neroli and cigarette smoke and coffee. And in this moment I am whole; I have never lost anything.

And soon we will sit down and order another atrocious wine and Mazita will say, "Here is Anna Irikina, the first poet of the City of the Plains!" And the crowd will be cheering and clapping, and Anna will stand up and walk to the stage, her chin high, and she will raise her hands and silence will fall, and she will say her poem into that listening silence, and it will pierce my heart. It will pierce my heart.

# 19

Mely is now a sleek black cat with impeccably white paws, but when she ran into my ankles in a blind, spitting panic in Kilok, she was a tiny ball of fluff with soft claws that could barely pierce the skin of my hands, no matter how she scratched. I picked her up and she opened her pink mouth and hissed at me. Her eyes, still filmed with the blue of kittenhood, were blazing with terror, and her fur was wet with her own piss.

I had spent a dispiriting morning trying to gather information at the Kilok market. I was not used to speaking to strangers; before I had always met people in my village, where I was an important person, and so I had been treated with respect. That day I began to discover what it means to be an unimportant person. I found it humiliating.

Because I looked like a river urchin, it was difficult to catch the attention of the traders, who would brush me off impatiently or simply ignore my presence. Even so, I had managed to ask a few people whether they had seen a woman like Jane Watson. One said she had: a fair-skinned woman had bought some almonds from her a week ago perhaps. But she didn't know where that woman might have gone, and had heard no talk of what she was doing. Another had been told of the woman with the silver camera and red hair, but had not seen her; he said that she was with a foreign man, and they had hired a jeep and gone into the desert. He asked me why I was looking for her, and I told him she owed me money, and it seemed for a moment that he had more to say. But then a customer wanted to buy some of his wares and he forgot about me. When I attempted to start the conversation again he waved me away, not even bothering to speak.

At least it seemed clear that Jane Watson was not in Kilok, but I hadn't found out anything at all useful. I wandered slowly back to the boat through the narrow alleyways, not really looking where I was going, and that's when Mely ran into my legs. I was so surprised I picked her up without thinking, and I held her tightly against my chest as she struggled and spat and scratched. (She is wrong when she remembers that she was too exhausted to scratch me.)

The last thing I'd expected to find in the lonely alleys of Kilok was a friend. Yet in those first moments, even before I was certain what kind of animal I was holding in my hands, I knew that Mely and I would be friends. Maybe it was just that my heart was bruised and hungry, and this frightened kitten seemed even more abject than I was, and my need flowered out to meet hers.

In any case, I stroked her until her body stopped trembling, and then I carried her back to the boat and gave her some of the sour goat's milk I had bought at the market. It didn't occur to me to do anything else. I thought vaguely that perhaps I could find out where she belonged in the morning, before I went downstream to the next village. But when I woke up and we shared breakfast, it seemed as if she were already part of where I was going. I asked her if she wanted to stay with me, and she stared at me with her mottled blue-green baby eyes and miaowed, and then she rubbed her chin on my hand and purred that loud, brambly kitten-purr. And that was that.

# 20

Today Mizan climbed the stairs to my flat, puffing and grumbling, to bring me a letter from my grandmother. For all his hard-fisted bargaining, he has a kind heart: in the three years since I reached the city, he has never failed to visit me in the autumn, after his long trek upriver, to give me news of my village. I am always glad to see his sweaty, pock-marked face. I can't offer him much for his trouble – a bottle of rice wine, some fresh bread, a meal of fish and dumplings – but he sits in my tiny kitchen on my thin, wobbly chair, Mely purring on his lap, and laughs his giant laugh, tearing hunks of bread with his big white teeth.

His visits always make me very homesick. I vividly remember other meals, other conversations, when he sat in state beside my mother and father in our house, thumping the table, making his terrible jokes. The first year, when I was still living in the shantytown, he asked me when I was planning to return home, and I didn't know what to say.

Mizan tells me gossip and news he gathers from his travels.

His journey grows more perilous every year, he says, and he is not sure how much longer he can keep going to my village. Things are getting worse month by month, week by week. He never travels without a gun and he has hired another man to guard his boat from looters and bandits. In one of the provinces in the mountains there is rebellion, and the army was sent from the city to hang the leaders. The people there are poor and desperate. In another the crime lords have taken over, and if Mizan wants to travel safely he has to pay money for protection.

I know I'm lucky to receive news from home. Some of my friends have no way of hearing from their families: they are tormented that they will never hear if someone they love has died, or is married, or has had children, or is suffering, or is happy. It is an ache in them that they never say. You learn very swiftly not to ask, or you wait until the shadows are soft and dark and the talk has become slow, and then you will be shown the precious photographs, thumbed and fading, of children who are now years older, of wives or husbands smiling at the camera in some far-off happier time. Then there are the photos or locks of hair of those whom they know they will never see again, because they are dead: killed in the accidents of war, or by hunger or disease. Their sorrow is delicate and huge, a cloud that lives inside them that no storm of tears will ever dissolve.

So Mizan is my angel, my messenger, and I am grateful. I write to my grandmother in the spring, and he takes my letter upriver. I tell her of my search for the Book, and of the friends I have made, and of my flat. I always try to sound cheerful. Her answer arrives in the autumn. She never asks about the Book. She writes a long letter, telling me all the major news of the year: important events, like the birth of Shiha's twins, and village news, like Sopli's accident with the axe, which left him with a missing finger, and the latest in the Juta family feud, and how Lila bought a new dinghy. I devour it all as if I am starving. I know my grandmother is trying to sound cheerful as well, and I know too that there is much that she is not saying. Both of us pretend that one day I will come home, and both of us know that I never will.

When Mizan left, I sat for a long time staring out of the window at the lamplight falling on the fig tree. What would I do if I went back to my village? If I returned without the Book, people would be sorry for me, and I couldn't bear that. It is much better to be anonymous, to lose myself in the river of the city, this great flow of people as nameless as I am. And now, when I have all but lost hope that I will ever see the Book again, I wonder if I would return even if I did find it. Would it be the same Book, or would it be damaged and changed, as I am? So many disrespectful hands must have opened it and touched its pages, so many eyes looked where they should not, and maybe its power has been violated and broken. Perhaps I could no longer speak to it, or it could no longer speak to me.

I think these things in the evenings when I am lonely and afraid, and the thoughts fill me with shame and doubt. Mely will sit on my lap then and say nothing, and her animal warmth is the single thing that shines in a world that seems to me to be without hope and without meaning.

# 21

The night after I found Mely, I slept soundly and woke early. I left almost as soon as I had broken my fast, pushing the boat into the middle of the river and then shipping the oars so I could just float along in the mild sun. Now I was leaving behind everything I knew. Kilok was as far downriver as I had ever been, and I left its boundaries with a feeling of trepidation and excitement. I felt that there ought to be a flourish of trumpets at such a momentous step, but the river looked just the same as it had before.

Mely didn't like the boat's motion, or the water lapping all around her. She crouched in the bottom, digging her claws into the wood and howling softly, until I picked her up and soothed her. Then she simply dug her claws into my lap, so I had tiny pink marks all over my thighs, but at least she stopped howling. In a very short time, however, she became used to the boat, and at last would sit on the prow for hours, staring into the river's ripples or ahead towards whatever was coming.

Over the next few days we visited a number of small

villages, which were like my home – motley collections of houses and orchards – but poorer. I always followed the same routine: I would hide my boat somewhere upstream and then, with Mely perched on my shoulder, I would make my investigations. People were often distrustful and wary, even when I wanted to buy food; sometimes someone would follow me from house to house, to make sure that I didn't steal anything. Refugees from upriver were a common sight here, and many were desperate enough to thieve. Even so, I also found kindness in unexpected places: the woman who invited me in for supper and sat me with her children and fed me bread fresh from her oven, impatiently waving away the coin I offered her, or the innkeeper who laughed uproariously when he saw the cat on my shoulder and gave me a meal for brightening up his day. It was then I noticed that those who have least often offer the most. I suppose they know what it was like to be hungry.

Despite everything, and not without a pang of guilt, I found I was enjoying myself. The weather was fine, neither too hot nor too cold, and now I had company. If I hadn't been so burdened with the search for the Book, I would have felt entirely carefree. I still found no word of Jane Watson: people remembered her on her trip upriver with Mizan, but had not seen her since. I began to wonder if she could perhaps make it overland to the city after all, although everyone said it was impossible because there was nothing but desert. I wished fiercely then that I could ask the Book for advice, or that I had asked the right questions when I had the chance. I knew my regrets were useless, and there seemed little choice but to go on.

I had been on the River for about a fortnight when Mely and I stopped at another small village. Without any hope of finding anything new, we wandered into the small space that passed for the village square. Instead of the usual population of a lean dog, a few scrawny chickens and an old man propped against a tree, there was a small crowd of people, and we could hear music. In the middle of all these people stood a boy with a *tar*. As we watched, he lifted his voice in song, and I realized it was the same boy I had heard singing on the bank on that first bleak morning in Kilok.

His voice seemed to soar out of his body as if it had nothing to do with him, as if he were not quite of this world. When he stopped singing, you saw that he was painfully shy: he shuffled his feet, scarcely able to look at the people who were now smiling and clapping. Blushing furiously, he pointed to his hat, which he had laid at his feet, and a few people threw in some coins. A small girl ran up and dropped in a big white radish, and ran off giggling. When it became clear that the boy wasn't going to sing any more, the crowd dispersed, leaving only Mely and me and a few uninterested chickens.

The boy examined his payment with a small shrug of disappointment, and then put his *tar* in its case. Me, I was burning with curiosity. What was this boy doing here? Why was he alone? Most of all, who was he? I went up to him and complimented him on his singing, and he blushed again and mumbled something.

"Didn't I see you in Kilok a couple of weeks ago?" I asked.

He looked at me properly this time. "Yes, I was in Kilok," he said. "I wasn't singing there, though."

I didn't want to confess that I had spied on him, and cast about for something to say, but now the boy was looking at Mely. "Why have you got a kitten on your shoulder?" he asked. "I've seen a man with a bird on his shoulder, but never a cat."

"This is Mely," I said. "She's my friend. And I'm Sim."

Mely stared at him and miaowed, and he tickled her under her chin until she started purring.

"I'm Yuri," he said. "I'm going to the city, because I heard they like singers there. I want to buy an electric guitar of my own."

He blushed, as if he had said more than he intended, but he had spoken so solemnly that I didn't dare to laugh, although I wanted to giggle at the sheer outrageousness of his ambition.

"I didn't know there were such things as electric *tars*," I said.

"*Guitar*, not *tar*," he said, with a trace of impatience. "They're like a *tar*, but they sing like nothing I've ever heard before. I'm going to sing and make money and buy one, and then I'll be famous."

I looked at him curiously, because I really didn't know what he was talking about. Then, with a care that suggested he was showing me his greatest treasure, he took a mobile phone out of his pocket. I didn't know what that was, either, until he explained. He pressed some buttons and it lit up, and then a tiny moving picture appeared in a screen on the front. It showed a man with an electric guitar, standing alone in a pool of garish light. Yuri only played it for a few seconds, and then turned it off: he said it would soon run out of power, and the phone was almost flat. The sound was fuzzy, but I could make it out: the man was singing, and the guitar was singing. The music sounded shiny and strange, but it moved me, and I looked at Yuri with quickening interest.

"I'm going to the city too," I said, on an impulse. "Why don't we travel together? I've got a boat."

His face lit up. "A boat?" he said. "I was thinking I might have to walk there…"

"You can't have walked from Kilok, surely?" I said.

"No, Old Yenni gave me a lift in his truck," he said. "But this was as far as he was going, and he left yesterday." Suddenly Yuri looked tired, and very young. "I don't have any money, and I don't know what to do, really. The city's much further than I thought."

I found myself staring in astonishment at this plump, tousle-haired boy. I thought he must be a bit simple: how could he have made such a momentous decision without first planning? Even I, ignorant as I was, had thought to bring food and money and clothes with me. It was as if he had just picked up his *tar* and left: and later I found out that was pretty much what he had done. But I was wrong to think that he was simple: it was more that his desire blazed inside him so fiercely that it left him little space for anything else. Yuri is as single-minded as any person I have ever met.

"Are you hungry?" I asked at last, for want of anything else to say.

"I have a radish," he said, holding it up and grinning. "How could I be hungry?"

"I have some food we can share," I said. "But I have to do some other things first. If you wait, we can eat soon."

Yuri trailed after me as I made my tour of the village, where I asked my questions and discovered that no one there had seen Jane Watson coming back downriver. Because of Yuri's singing, we were both invited for a meal with the village elder. There was rice wine and goat stew and afterwards there was music. Mely sat in my lap and purred as we sang the old, beautiful songs, and then we took our leave and stumbled out into the star-filled night.

22

Yuri might have been a river boy, but he was not much at ease in boats. He clambered in like a landsman and sat uncomfortably in the middle, clutching his *tar* and bag, and gulped as I steered us mid-river. As we had not much else to do to pass the time, he told me his story. He had been orphaned at an early age, and since then had lived with his uncle in Kilok, who, it seemed, had not a lot of patience or kindness to spare for a fat, clumsy boy with little talent for anything except daydreaming and making music.

"He didn't like me much," Yuri said. "He'd just sigh and go, *Tch tch*, and tell me how much I was costing him. If I could have been good at fishing or something, he might have forgiven me." But Yuri was disastrously bad at most tasks: he fell out of boats, he fell out of trees, he spilled buckets of milk, he let the goats eat the barley. Punishment made no difference, and at last his uncle just shrugged and let him alone.

If his uncle had had more imagination, he might have apprenticed Yuri to a musician, but it never occurred to him to do so: music was strictly for the evening, after the day's work was finished, and he didn't believe it was work. If it hadn't been for Jane Watson, Yuri said, he might have stayed in Kilok his whole life. At this, my ears pricked up.

"It's funny you were asking questions about her," he said. "Miss Watson came to Kilok and spoke to my uncle. She was nice. My uncle made me sing her a song, and then she gave me the phone and showed me the electric guitars and told me about the music in her country, and how singers could be very rich, even here, in the city. I thought about it all for a long time after she had left, and I wondered why I couldn't be rich too, if I went to the city and became a singer. Then I could pay back my uncle all the money I have cost him, and have my own house. And then Old Yenni said he was driving downriver, so I asked if I could come too. And here I am."

For a while I sat silent, struck by how Jane Watson had so lightly changed our lives. Did she ever think about the effects of her actions? She must have known that to steal an object like the Book would be devastating to our whole village, but that knowledge hadn't stopped her. To me, this seemed to be the very definition of wrong. With Yuri, her actions seemed equally wrong, but in a different way.

She must have seen that Yuri was unhappy; she must have recognized his talent. Most likely it never occurred to her what her casual gift might mean to Yuri. I don't doubt she wished to please him, just as she pleased the children in our village by taking photos and showing them what they looked like on the small screen in her silver camera. She had tossed a bomb into Yuri's world and then sailed off without another thought. I was stunned by her carelessness. At the same time, who was I to say she was wrong, when Yuri's desire to make music burned inside him so fiercely, yet found no answer where he was?

I didn't tell Yuri why I was searching for Jane Watson,

beyond the fact that she had taken something that I wanted back, and he didn't ask. He accepted everything without question, which confirmed my impression of him as a harmless simpleton. He was so different from my lively, curious brothers and sisters, who, if they had been living in such close quarters with me, would have found out in less than a day that I wasn't the boy I claimed to be. He never once peeped when I told him to look away because I was doing my personal business, and he never asked why I wanted to be so private. It wasn't until later that I reflected that maybe life had taught him not to ask questions.

Yuri was right about his incompetence. He was no help at all on the boat and sometimes, in those first few days, I thought I must have been mad to ask him to join us. I tried not to be testy with him, but it was hard when he dropped an oar and I had to dive in and retrieve it, or when he stood up clumsily and nearly tipped us over. I began to feel a sneaking sympathy for Yuri's uncle. Yet it wasn't that the boy didn't want to help: all his accidents stemmed from his over-eagerness, and he looked so humiliated when things went wrong that I bit my tongue. Eventually, I found that if I showed him how to do things patiently, step by step, he didn't make so many mistakes, though he was still apt to daydream and forget what he was supposed to be doing.

It was during our visits to the villages along the River that our strange partnership began to bear fruit. Instead of waiting for villagers to throw coins into Yuri's hat, I carried it around from person to person, smiling and bowing, and this increased takings considerably. Very often we were both invited for meals by people anxious to hear Yuri sing again. This was welcome, because my food stocks were getting low and my money was dwindling faster than I had expected. I had thought that I might be able to earn more as I travelled, but my skills were in reading and weaving, which nobody needed, and few people could afford to pay for farm work. So it turned out that meeting Yuri was lucky for both of us. We helped each other, as waifs do, and learned how to survive.

# 23

Perhaps it sounds strange, but I think fondly of that part of our journey. I remember the boat floating gently down the river, Yuri idly plucking the *tar*, Mely crouched on the prow with her kitten fur fluffed out, and the sun shining over us all. The riverbanks slid past us, the dun plains stretched as far as the eye could see. Mely liked Yuri and spent a lot of time purring on his lap while I was busy keeping us away from the banks. Sometimes, drifting down the River on late-summer evenings, I realized with a start of guilt that I felt entirely happy. It was so very peaceful, with the fragrance of desert grasses floating over the water, and the first stars beginning to flower, and the cries of the curlews winding through Yuri's music, that for a while I even forgot about the Book. I always rebuked myself sternly for these lapses, but perhaps it was not so wrong of me.

There was little river traffic: a few small traders like my father, a few fishermen. When we passed them, we would put our hands up and nod, acknowledging each other as fellow travellers on the water roads. Even though this country was beyond my knowledge, it wasn't very different from the lands in which I'd been raised: the same kinds of villages with the same gods and courtesies, the same goats gathered on the bank, chewing as they watched us float past.

There was much I didn't know, but I had read a description in the Book about the downstream course of the River, and Mizan had told me about some of his adventures. This meant I was not entirely ignorant. I knew that after it left the high Plains of Pembar, the River flowed into the Lorban Mountains. The Book had said that these were fabled for their loveliness, and were home to many gods, with many sacred places. Mizan said that the River through the Lorban Valley was deep and wide and strong, surrounded by tall, rocky mountains that were often wreathed in mist, and that it would rain there even in summer.

"There are reasons why my boat has a big engine, young Sim," he'd say. "It needs to be strong and heavy, so it is not swept away on the current and smashed on rocks. It is a long way to the Plains of Pembar! And that is why I can sell your cloth for a good price, because it is so hard to get. And pay you a good price too," he added.

(I discovered when I reached the city that Mizan sold our cloth for a very good price indeed, a hundred times above what he paid us: when I taxed him with this, he smiled and said, "But I have expenses, Sim. We all have to live, eh? I take the trouble to come west every year. I take the trouble to bargain. Nobody thought I underpaid them in your village, eh? You were all pleased with what I paid." That was true enough. And even though I thought he was cheating my people, I found I still couldn't dislike him.)

We saw the Lorban Mountains first as distant purple smudges on the horizon. Day by day, the banks grew steeper and the river grew narrower and faster. It was as if the River was eager to reach the mountains: it seemed to gather up its skirts and run towards them. I had to pay special attention so we did not get into trouble. Of course Yuri was no help at all, and Mely just crouched in the middle of the boat, complaining softly and trying to keep dry. We swirled into the Lorban Gorge like leaves on a gale. My ears were suddenly stuffed full: the air pressure shifted, there was mist everywhere, the song of the River echoed back from the rocky sides of the gorge and the mountains rose around us like the grey flanks of a huge animal.

For the first time since I had left home, it rained. I had a skin to put over the boat, which meant we were damp rather than soaked, but it was a fragile protection against the freezing cold. Water gathered in the bottom of the boat and had to be bailed out, and my bag and all my spare clothes were soaked through. The riverbanks were sheer rock, and for the first night in the mountains it was impossible to get out onto the shore. I didn't sleep at all for fear we would capsize. All night long I made the songs my father had taught me, to keep us safe in the currents of the river spirit. I don't know if the River heard me, but somehow we survived those first rapids unspilled, bursting out of the narrow gorge into a wide, forested valley late the next day.

That night I saw the face of the River god, sad and tormented, rising through the darkness and foam like a drowning girl. I heard her singing of the acid rains and the rising salt and the poisons that ran down from the cotton fields and the silt that killed her fish. I felt the lament for a damaged future rise through my bones, from my chilled feet to the top of my skull. I heard her tell me that nothing would ever be the same again.

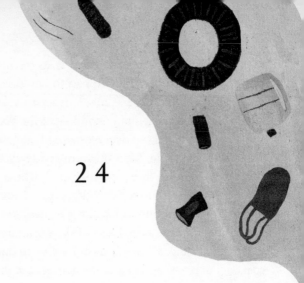

# 2 4

Mely asked me today why I keep writing this book. I was surprised by her question, and thought about it for some time. I want, I told her, to tell my story to someone, even if it is only Mely who hears it. Mely pointed out that I could just say it to her, without all the bother of scratching the pen over the paper, and cursing at my mistakes, and having to start again. "I would listen," she said. "I like to listen to you."

So then I said that I write because I miss the Book and in some way want to replace it, impossible though that might be. But that seems like a great vanity to me: nothing will replace the Book. Although I've done my best, I still think I have not been able to explain the abyss its absence has left in my being. Maybe I will never be able to. I know people who have lost their homes and whose families have all died: for me, the loss of the Book is of that order, although I would never say so to them, for fear of being misunderstood. Some people might think it callous of me to equate the loss of an object with the loss of a loved person, but that is how it feels to me.

Even though I know that writing my story each night will never replace the Book, it does stop the missing I feel inside me, even if it is only for a short time. But is that why I sit down each night and struggle so to put these things down on paper?

I told Mely that I hoped that I might make something beautiful. I told her that I hope to remember what is lost. I said that I hope to discover something, to become what I might be. That's why I sit here in the lamplight at my tiny kitchen table, and write one word after another. When I wake in the morning and read what I wrote the night before, it is never what I had hoped. It seems to me to be a tinny echo, when what I felt was a glorious symphony of sound and colour and feeling. Remnants, shadows, fragments. Is that all I have left?

Maybe the strangest thing is that I don't know any more what it is that I am hoping for.

Mely looked at me with her clear green eyes and swished her tail and yawned her delicate yawn.

"Why do you do it, really?" she asked.

And I realized I didn't have an answer.

# 25

Last night, Ling Ti dropped by unexpectedly to visit me, on his way home from reading his poems at the university. He had told us not to bother to come, as the other poets would be dull and we could hear his poetry any time we liked. When Ling Ti says things like that, he means it – he always tells us if he wants us to be there – so I had stayed at home. I was tired from work, and it was raining, and I had thought I might write something. Ling Ti halted in the doorway when he saw my book and pen on the table, lying in the circle of the lamplight. "I'm interrupting you," he said. "I can come another time."

In truth I had been sitting at the table for half an hour, sucking the end of the pen and wondering where to begin. Sometimes my mind is completely blank; or maybe there are too many things, and I don't know which one to pick. Many nights I don't write anything at all.

"You're not interrupting anything important," I said. "Please stay. I have some rice wine, if you would like some?"

"I've already had enough to drink," said Ling Ti. "I think I'd prefer some tea."

He sat down and watched as I lit the gas ring and boiled a saucepan of water. He amused me by telling me about his reading. He had intended to be polite, or so he said, because the university paid well, and he needed the money. But one of the other poets had told him afterwards that his poetry lacked soul, and so Ling Ti had told him what he thought about *his* poems. "Soul!" said Ling Ti. "What would that centipede know about soul? He thinks it's all about looking at the moon and thinking about a beautiful woman and feeling a bit sad. Pap!" The upshot was, he said, that he would probably never be asked to read there again.

I could see him glancing at my book, which was open on the table. I wanted to hide it, as if I had been discovered doing something embarrassing, but putting it away would only have served to draw more attention. It's not that my story is a big secret, but I feel shy about telling anyone, especially Anna or Ling Ti, who are real poets.

Mely, who had been asleep on my bed, wandered into the kitchen, yawning ostentatiously to show that she wasn't curious at all about who had come to visit. When she saw it was Ling Ti, she rubbed herself against his long legs until he picked her up and put her on his lap, where she curled up and purred.

Mely approves of Ling Ti: he and Yuri are the only people she will talk to, aside from me. Anna and Icana don't like cats. Although they have made a special exception for Mely, and have even invited both of us to their apartment, Mely is still a bit offended.

"I didn't know you wrote, Sim," said Ling Ti, as I handed him a cup of tea. "Is it a book?"

I felt myself going hot all over. "Not really," I said. "I'm writing down my story. It's not a proper book, not like what you and Anna write."

Mely looked up, her green eyes flashing. "Of course it's a proper book," she said. "It's just as proper as silly poems."

Ling Ti laughed at that and poked Mely in the tummy. "Watch it, you impertinent animal," he said. "I didn't mean to embarrass you, Sim. I was just being nosy. You don't have to tell me anything. I hate talking about what I am writing. Though I can talk about it when it's finished. *Then* I can talk for hours, even if it's all lies."

Once he said that, I found that I could speak about my book, after all. Ling Ti listened attentively, sipping his tea and tickling Mely's chin until she fell asleep again. In the end, I told him all about the Book, and Jane Watson, and my village. I had told him bits here and there, of course, but never the whole story. His response surprised me.

"But you must write it down," he said to me. "And never say again that it isn't important. Never. Not to anyone."

"Would you read a book like that?" I asked.

"I would read anything you wrote," he said.

I laughed. "I could be the worst writer in the world," I said. "How can you tell if it would be worth reading?"

He paused, and gave me a narrow look. "I'm not patronising you, Sim. I just think you are truthful, and I know the way you speak. I would like to read a story that you wrote."

I hadn't imagined before that anyone might read this book, aside from me and Mely. The thought gave me butterflies. "Maybe I'm not writing it for anybody to read," I said. "Maybe it's just private."

"All writing comes from the inside," said Ling Ti. "It burns you with wanting to be written. It's the writing that matters. You don't have to show it to anybody if you don't want to." He grinned at me. "I choose to, of course, because I am a great poet, and I wish to share my greatness with everybody."

Ling Ti always jokes about being a great poet. The biggest

joke, as Anna says, is that he probably *is* a great poet. He says it to annoy other poets, especially those he says are mangy weasels who wouldn't know a real poem if they tripped over it. (Actually, what he says is much ruder than that.) He argues with other writers all the time, and because of that many people are a little afraid of him. I was, until I began to know him better.

A comfortable silence fell between us. I studied his face, which was serious and gentle in the mild lamplight. It's an expression he never reveals except to his close friends. In public, Ling Ti is a showman: he gets away with being a mischief-maker because he makes people laugh. His poems are ironic and abrasive and angry and full of dazzle. Those who admire them say they are beautiful, and even his enemies find it hard to deny their intelligence. But there's something else underneath, something quieter and deeper, that people sense and respond to. It's why his poems matter.

As if he could hear my thoughts, Ling Ti looked up at me, pushing his glasses up his nose. "The secret, Sim, is always to write with love," he said. "Love is the hardest thing in the world, and it's the one thing we mustn't forget. It's much more difficult than anyone thinks. I believe that you know that already, and that's why I would like to read your book."

It is unusual for Ling Ti to give anyone a compliment, and I suddenly felt very shy, although it also pleased me. He saw that I was uncomfortable and changed the subject, and we chatted about this and that, and then he went home. After he left, I thought about what he had said. Maybe he is right. Maybe it is love that makes me want to write this story.

# 2 6

I discovered a lot about people on our journey to the city. Not all of it was good. I remember the people who turned us away with blows when we were in need, or who cheated us, charging us ten or twenty times what we should have paid, because they knew we had no choice but to buy from them. But then I remember Mei, the innkeeper in the mountains, who let us stay for a week when we turned up at her doorstep, woeful and drenched, after our boat sprang a leak halfway through the Lorban Mountains.

I don't know why she took pity on us: she was tough and unsentimental and, from what I saw, a ruthless business-woman. And yet she fed us and gave us a room in her attic, briskly refusing our poor payment. When Yuri offered to sing in her bar, as some kind of return, she shrugged and said he could if he liked. He did, and after the first night word spread, and her bar was full every evening following, which pleased her. But she gave us a room before she knew of Yuri's talent, and called a carpenter to repair our boat, and loaded us with food supplies when we left, pooh-poohing any of our stumbling attempts at thanks or payment.

By then, we did not expect kindness from strangers. I thought of Kular sitting at our table in tears, telling us that he had forgotten that people could be kind, and reflected sadly that I now knew what he meant. I forgave those in want or fear, because I understood why they closed their faces against us, but it's less easy to forgive those to whom a bed in a stable or a piece of bread was no trespass on their need. And yet people were kind to us, sometimes when we least expected it.

It took us two months to reach the city, and we arrived just before the coldest part of the winter. I sometimes wonder that we got here at all, although the truth is that we were never in serious danger. There was a lot of rain and discomfort and cold and hunger, but nothing that directly threatened our lives; nobody, not even Yuri, found out that I was not a boy, nobody tried to rob us of our few possessions, or to kidnap us, or to kill us. For the most part nobody noticed us at all.

We left the mountains and found ourselves in the plains that surround the city. Now the River was wide and lazy and full of traffic, and the water changed colour. We passed factories that poured out black smoke and leaked stinking liquids, red or black or sickly yellow, and wide broken drains that poured sewage and rubbish into the water. After both of us spent two days vomiting, we no longer dared to drink the water, and had to buy it in bottles.

We stayed nowhere for longer than a night. I still asked after Jane Watson, but there was no news: the presence of a foreigner was not so notable here. The hopelessness I had begun to feel in the mountains took hold inside me. I felt heavy with it, as if my bones were made of lead. Those were the worst days, when I could no longer see any point in continuing the journey, but couldn't face returning home with empty hands.

When we finally reached the city, we felt neither relief nor gladness. Our first sight of the slums and shanties crowded at the edges shocked us. We were used to living among people who owned very little, but this was something we hadn't seen before. Yet even there, among the filth and crowded despair and disease and hardship, we found kindness. Even there.

# 27

Yuri is quite famous now. He started singing in bars when we were living in the shantytown, and word spread, and then he got a regular spot at the Stray Dog. He saved up and bought his electric guitar, and then he had to save up some more so he could live in a house that had electricity so he could practise. I laughed at him for a long time when he came to me, wholly cast down because he couldn't play his new possession: it was so typical of him. Luckily for Yuri, Mazita has taken over his business affairs, since he would be as helpless as a baby chick without someone to manage him. All he thinks about is his music: he doesn't care for money or fame, except for the fact that they allow him to play what he wants.

I still smile when I remember the moment I finally revealed that I was really a girl, although it was so very painful. It was when we first reached the city and had no money to speak of, and were living on what we could earn through Yuri's singing and odd jobs I picked up here and there, running errands or sorting through rubbish for what could be reused or (once, because I only lasted a day) working in a smelter in the shanty-town, stoking a furnace. Yuri and I had been together for weeks at this point, and I was privately astonished that he had never worked out that I was not a boy. I began to feel worse and worse about deceiving him; if he had asked, I would have confessed straight away, but he never asked. So one evening, I just told him.

At first Yuri flatly refused to believe me, and I began to wonder, in a slightly panic-stricken way, what I would have to do to convince him. Would I be forced to take off all my clothes? For the first time, I told him the full story of Jane Watson and the Book, and my full name. I told him about my mother and my grandmother, and why I had left my village. He listened in silence, his face deepening to a dull red flush. I thought he was very angry with me, and kept talking anxiously, hoping that his anger would pass. Finally I ran out of things to say and found myself sitting in dejected silence.

At last he spoke. "But I can't talk to girls!" he said.

I was very taken aback. "I'm a girl," I said. "And you can talk to me."

"You weren't a girl before," he said. "You were just like me. How can I talk to you now? You're a girl! And you *lied* to me."

"I really didn't mean to lie to you, and it was very wrong of me," I said. "But I've never lied about anything else. I'm exactly the same person you've always known. And anyway, why should me being a girl make any difference?"

"I don't know," he mumbled. "It just does. It's … humiliating."

I saw he was very upset and didn't know how to answer him. I thought that we were both right, and that it did and did not make a difference.

"I mean – girls giggle and make fun of you because you're fat," he said. "What if you start doing that, now you're a girl?"

I stared at him. "I've been a girl all along; I haven't just changed into one. And do you really think I would do that?"

"That's what girls do," he said.

"Some girls," I said. "*Some* girls. I bet boys were cruel to you too."

"Yes, but they were boys. They just punched me and called me names. They didn't giggle."

Some cruel imp in me wanted to giggle then, out of sheer nervousness, but I dared not.

"Yuri," I said sternly, "I'm Sim. I'm just me. Everybody is just who they are, just like you are just you. Whether I'm a girl or not doesn't make any difference. I wouldn't punch you if I were a boy. I won't giggle at you because I'm a girl. I'm your *friend*."

I studied him as he sat glowering and silent, biting his lip, and my heart began to hurt. "I don't have any other friends, aside from Mely," I said, my voice wavering. "Don't you want to be my friend any more?"

Yuri glanced up then, and saw that I was on the edge of tears. He looked astonished. I think it had never occurred to him before that anybody could actually like him. He said nothing for a long time, and then he said gruffly that of course he was my friend. After a few days, he even said he didn't mind my being a girl.

Along with Mely, Yuri is my closest friend; we see each other almost every day, as he lives not far from me. He is no longer the shy, awkward boy I first met: he has grown to be handsome, and has discovered that there are many girls besides me who won't tease him. Through Yuri I met Icana and Anna and Ling Ti, and they invite me to their apartments and introduce me to other people. I now know more people than I ever knew in my own village; some are little more than strangers, but we recognize and greet each other.

The city is very different from my village, where everybody had known everybody else all their lives, and a new face was a novelty. Sometimes I find knowing so many people overwhelming and confusing. When I told Anna this, she laughed and ruffled my hair and said I was still a country girl at heart. I think she is right: I will never be at home in the city, not like someone who was born here. And yet, how much poorer my life would have been if I hadn't met my crazy friends! I love them for their jokes and their generosity and their outrageous clothes and their passionate arguments, and I love the beautiful things they make, and most of all I love their quick and tactful understanding when I am sad. They are true companions. How could I wish that I had never met them?

Yuri seems much less troubled by the city than I am, but he was never happy at home: for him, his new life is miraculous. Me, I miss too many things.

# 28

I was hurrying home through the Financial District today after I had closed my stall, when I saw Jane Watson. I glimpsed her out of the corner of my eye, and it was as if an electric shock went through my whole body. It's been weeks since I asked anyone about her, and months since I hoped to see her ever again.

Her face was on a bank of television screens in a shop window, flickering and discoloured. She was talking to someone in a yellow studio, seated on an elegant red chair. Jane Watson was speaking in her own language and there were subtitles underneath the picture, so that even though the sound was turned down, I could read what was being said. The interviewer said she was a famous scholar who had spent some months in our country, researching the traditional folkways of our people. Jane Watson looked very serious and said that an ancient way of life was under threat. She talked about the cotton fields and the problems with the River. There were tears in her eyes as she spoke about how a beautiful way of life was dying, and how the simple

River people didn't understand what was happening to them.

I felt a lurch in my stomach when she said that, as if I were going to be sick. My people are not simple. There are things they don't understand, but that doesn't mean that they are stupid or even ignorant. I watched, fascinated and repulsed, waiting for Jane Watson to mention the Book: but she didn't talk about it at all.

Jane Watson had written her own book. It was called *The River People of the Pembar Plains*. The interviewer held it up so everyone could see. On the cover was a photograph of me, taken on the day that she came to our village. I went hot all over with embarrassment: I was wearing my best clothes that day, with my hair carefully braided, but in the bright yellow light of the television studio I just looked quaint and poor, an ignorant peasant. The interviewer asked who I was, and she told him I was one of the daughters of the headman of the village, and that she had become friends with me while she stayed in our home. I felt my stomach clench with rage: my father was important because he was married to a Keeper, not the other way around. I had thought she understood that. She said the photograph showed the dignity my people maintained, even though they lived in such poverty. She didn't tell the interviewer my name or my title, and she didn't mention my grandmother at all.

For a while I was so angry that I forgot to read the subtitles, and when I started paying attention again, the interviewer was talking to the camera and Jane Watson had disappeared and the television flickered to advertisements.

I don't know how long I stood outside that window as people pushed past me in the twilight, cursing me for blocking the footpath. My whole body was shaking with fury. I wondered how she dared to put my photograph on the cover of her book, knowing what she had done to me. I wondered how she could cry over my village, when she had stolen its most precious treasure. I wondered what kind of person could lie like that and not feel ashamed of themselves. I wondered if she even knew that she was lying.

In the shantytowns I have spoken to women who have been raped, and they told me how they felt, how the most intimate and fragile sense of themselves had been torn open and violated. I think it is wrong of me to take their terrible experiences and compare them to mine, but I can't help it. That is how I felt when I saw Jane Watson on the television. I felt as if my soul had been violated.

# 29

I dreamed of my grandmother last night. In my dream, she wasn't old: she was young, as young as my mother was when I was a little girl. I was a crane, and I was flying over my village. The plains stretched out beneath my wings, in all their subtle and various colours. People think of the plains as empty and harsh, but they are wrong; the land quivers with life. The grasses in my dream flowered in soft colours, purple and pink and yellow, and small herds of deer looked up as my shadow passed over them, and hares startled and ran. I could hear the music of crickets and grasshoppers rising up in the warm air, and I smelled the grass, fresh and wild.

Grandmother was standing outside our house with her arms raised, singing to welcome me to the village. It was a song I didn't know, and I thought it was the most beautiful melody I had ever heard. When I woke up, I tried to remember it, but it vanished away with most of the dream.

When she saw me, Grandmother smiled. She knew it

was me. She waited while I circled down and perched on the chimney of our house.

"Welcome, Simbala Da Kulafir Atan Mucarek Abaral Effenda Nuum," she said. "It's good to see you."

"Hello, Grandmother," I said. "I am a crane now. Do you mind?"

Grandmother laughed. "Of course I don't mind," she said. "I always knew you were a crane. But don't forget us, eh?"

"How could I forget you?" I said. "I miss you all the time."

"My name is in your name," said Grandmother. "And your daughter will be all our names too."

As she said that, I saw that my mother was standing beside her, and then I saw a crowd of other women, and I knew they belonged to me. There was my great-grandmother, Mucarek, and my great-great-grandmother, Abaral, and many others I couldn't name. They were dressed in their best clothes, and the sun shone down on all the colours so that I was dazzled. I blinked, and then they were all gone, all my mothers, and the village was empty. And then everything faded away and vanished before my eyes.

I dreamed some other things I don't remember, and when I woke up, my face was cold with tears.

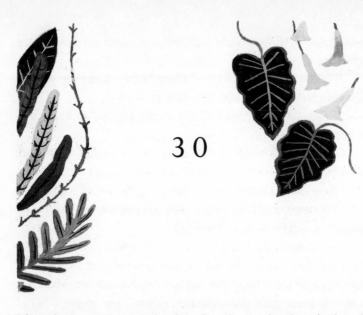

# 3 0

I bought Jane Watson's book today. It was hard to find and expensive, but if I am careful this month I will not be too much out of pocket. Ling Ti offered to steal it for me, as he said I should not give Jane Watson my money by buying her book, but I told him that would be unfair to the bookshop. It hasn't been translated, and I can read it only with the greatest difficulty. Ling Ti speaks that language fluently, and he said he would read it for me and then condemn it in the literary magazine that publishes his poems.

I said that perhaps he shouldn't make his mind up about what he thinks before he reads the book, but he is adamant that Jane Watson should be torn limb from limb. "Not literally, of course," he said, pushing his glasses up his nose and grinning. "Just in a very bloody, metaphorical way." He made me laugh for the first time in days.

Ling Ti spends half his time writing furious editorials designed to upset his poetic enemies. When I ask him why, he usually says he does it for fun. If he's very drunk, he tells me that it's because the world needs to be cleansed of buffoons and shysters, and that he is the Broom of Truth. Icana worries that he will get into trouble with the authorities, but he just laughs and takes no notice. I worry too. There are many poets in prison here, and even more who have been forced to live in exile.

Me, I find that I am not interested in making the Book an occasion for some kind of silly feud. And I am determined to read Jane Watson's book for myself, no matter how difficult it is. Perhaps she has written something about my Book that might help me to find it. But I think, more than anything, that I am hoping to discover why she did what she did. I think not understanding how she could have betrayed us like that haunts me almost as much as the loss of the Book itself.

Mely, of course, doesn't know why I am bothering. She says I should either track down Jane Watson and demand the Book back, or just accept that it is gone and get on with making sure I earn enough money for our treats. She is very angry that I can't afford to buy chicken this month.

# 31

It is a long time since I last wrote here: a month at least. I've scarcely seen most of my friends. The last time I talked to Yuri was ten days ago. We shared a quick glass of bubble tea, and when I stood up to go home he complained that he never sees me any more. I told him I was too busy reading and he made a face and said that I had better finish soon.

For weeks I've been spending my evenings struggling with Jane Watson's book. It wasn't just that it was hard to read because I don't know the language very well; it also made me feel things I didn't expect.

Before I read any of the text, I looked at all the photographs. Only a few were of my village. Jane Watson had taken pictures of people all along the River. Some of them made me smile: Mizan, leaning on the rails of his boat, grinning into the camera; and Mei, the innkeeper in the mountains who was kind to Yuri and me, standing in the doorway of her house, her worn hands on her broad hips. Some of the photographs were very beautiful, and some of them were very sad;

but they all seemed long ago and far away.

I don't know what to say about Jane Watson's book. I have found out things I didn't know: she describes the foreign companies that are financing the cotton fields, and names the insecticides that are poisoning the river water, and there are tables of figures that show how much water is being taken from the River. She writes about how the government has sent troops to protect the cotton fields from angry locals, and the corruption that has made it possible for land to be stolen from people who had farmed it for generations.

She talks about the violence that Kular described to us, long, long ago in our kitchen. Jane Watson tells it as if she standing at a distance, looking from above like an eagle, so she can observe patterns and connections that can't be seen at ground level. She writes about rivers that have died in other parts of the world, and warns that the same thing will happen to our River, which feeds the whole country from the Plains of Pembar to the city. She quotes scientists and sociologists and ecologists and politicians. She talks about the suffering of the village people, of how they are driven from their homes by violence and famine, to end up in the shantytowns that cluster around the city.

It is much more interesting than what she said on the television, and, despite everything, I reluctantly admire what she has done. When I got to the end of the book, I turned it over and looked at the cover: my face gazed back at me under the title, but somehow it wasn't my face any more, just as the story Jane Watson tells isn't my story. It belongs to so many people, but somehow it seems to me to belong most of all to Jane Watson. I heard her hard, cool voice in my head, putting together her facts and her arguments. She was very convincing. She said she is fighting for justice. She is telling the world about what is happening to my people, just as she said she would all those long months ago when first I met her. All the same, something important is missing among all those facts and figures and quotations, although I can't put my finger on what it is.

I remember what Mely said when she objected to me writing about her. *I'm not a story,* Mely told me. *I'm your friend. What if you say things that aren't true? Won't you be changing how things are?* Has Jane Watson changed things by writing her book? Maybe things had already changed before I realized, and she was just what followed.

There is one missing thing that is easy to spot. In all the hundreds of pages of *The River People of the Pembar Plains*, Jane Watson doesn't mention the Book. Not once. I read it through twice to be sure. She writes about the temple and the harvest and the weaving and the river traffic, noticing all sorts of details, but in her story the Keepers don't exist. For a terrible moment I wondered whether I had imagined everything: perhaps the Book was just a story my mother and grandmother had told me and that I had childishly believed was real. Maybe it had never existed at all. But I remembered my name. I said it out loud: Simbala Da Kulafir Atan Mucarek Abaral Effenda Nuum. It tells who I am, and who my mother and her mother were, right back to my great-great-grandmother.

Even if the Book is lost for ever, even if no one but me remembers it, we are the Keepers.

# 3 2

In the weeks when I was reading Jane Watson's book, Ling Ti dropped in every few days to find out how it was going. He would sit in my kitchen with Mely purring on his lap, the lamplight shining on the lenses of his glasses, and demand to know what I had read, and what I thought of it. He behaved like a teacher who was giving a lesson. He listened intently. I don't think anybody I know listens as hard as Ling Ti. When what I said didn't make sense, because I had misread something or I didn't know the meanings of the words, he would take the book and read out the passage, and we would talk it over until I understood it. I asked him once why he bothered, and he said that it mattered, that what was happening to the River people was important, and what happened to me was important too. I asked him if he was still planning to write an editorial that would tear Jane Watson limb from limb, and he replied that he wasn't sure any more if that was the right thing to do.

He visited the day after I had finished reading. I told him then that Jane Watson hadn't mentioned the Book or the

Keepers, and how it had made me feel. Ling Ti screwed up his face. "Would you have felt better if she had?" he asked.

The question surprised me, and so I thought about it before I replied. "It might have made me feel worse," I said. "She would have been writing about something she didn't understand at all. She would have got it wrong."

"Perhaps she was being tactful, because she knew she didn't understand it," said Ling Ti. "Or perhaps she didn't think it was relevant, compared to what is happening to the River."

It sounded as if he were defending her.

"The Book was the most precious thing in our village," I said indignantly. "How could she pretend it didn't exist? It was disrespectful. Especially to my grandmother. Jane Watson didn't seem to think that she mattered at all." I didn't add: it was disrespectful to *me*, but I meant that too.

Ling Ti frowned, and was silent for a while, so the only sound in the kitchen was the popping of the oil lamp and Mely's purr. Then he looked at me, and I saw that his face was unusually serious.

"Sim," he said, "Jane Watson is here, in the city. She is staying at the university for a year, as a guest, and I know how to find her."

For a few moments I couldn't breathe. "Jane Watson?" I said, stupidly. "Here?"

"Yes. I could take you to visit her, and you could ask her about the Book yourself."

It seemed to me that Ling Ti looked slightly guilty as he said this.

"You've known for a while, haven't you?" I said.

"A couple of weeks," he said. "I ... wanted to be sure before I told you. I know people in the faculty, and they put us in touch. She wants to interview me."

"Why?" I said blankly.

Ling Ti smiled. "Because I am a great poet, of course. I thought I could take you too."

After all this time, after all my long searching, I almost refused. I told Ling Ti that the last person I ever wanted to see was Jane Watson. I was filled with a consuming anger. I stood up and threw the book at Ling Ti and shouted that he should have told me before, that he should have warned me, that I didn't want his stupid help, sticking his stupid nose into my business. Mely yowled and ran out of the room. I pummelled Ling Ti's chest with my fists and he was forced to hold me back so I wouldn't hurt him. He just said my name, over and over again, until I calmed down; and then I burst into tears, and he held me until I stopped crying.

"Sim," he said again, and he wiped the tears from my cheeks with his fingers. Then he kissed me. No man has ever kissed me before, and for a little while I forgot all about Jane Watson and my village and the Book. I forgot about everything except Ling Ti.

# 33

I feel raw, as if all my feelings have come to the surface of my skin and there is nothing to protect me from them. It's because at last I will speak to Jane Watson, but it is also because of Ling Ti. He told me that he hadn't meant to kiss me that day, but that he had wanted to ever since we met. "I didn't know how," he said to me yesterday. "You are so prickly, Sim."

"Me?" I said. "Prickly? What about you? You fight with almost everyone you know."

"That's because I am a great poet," he said.

"You are also the vainest person I know," I said.

"You know it's true."

"You're not greater than Anna."

"That's true too," he said, smiling. "It's all nonsense, anyway."

Anna and Icana had known how Ling Ti felt all along, and when we walked into the Stray Dog holding hands, their faces lit up and they clapped. Icana says that is because they are sentimental romantics and they couldn't help hoping that one day

122

I would see that we belonged together. Anna says she mostly wanted us to get together because I am the only possible cure for Ling Ti's vanity. They teased us, which made me feel awkward, but then the music started and we danced and I forgot all about being shy. At this time, in this place, I am happy. It is a happiness that is threaded through with a terrible sadness: I have lost so much, and found so much, and it's hard to disentangle one thing from the other.

Mely is jealous. She didn't speak to me for two days, but fortunately she likes Ling Ti too much to stay angry. For those two days, she made my life miserable. She refused to eat or to come into the flat, and hid in the fig tree, sulking. Ling Ti was cunning and brought some chicken livers over, and we left them on the sill as we sat in the kitchen talking. Mely can't resist chicken livers, and it wasn't long before we saw her in the tree, her nose twitching. We pretended we hadn't noticed her, and step by step she crept to the window, until she was hunched on the closest branch. She was very hungry, but she is also very stubborn, and she knew that if she ate the livers, she would have to forgive us. She sat on that branch for more than half an hour. In the end she came back inside, and when she had eaten the livers she pretended that she hadn't been offended, after all. "I have been very busy," she told me haughtily. "I have lots of friends you don't know about."

Now she says it will be all right as long as everything remains the same. The problem is that nothing ever does.

Last night all my dearest friends came over: Anna and Icana and Yuri and Ling Ti. It was a wonderful evening. I made my favourite rice dish and everyone brought wine and sweets, and we sat on the carpet on cushions and gossiped and joked. When we had finished eating, we talked for a long time about Jane Watson.

Ling Ti has made an appointment to visit her next week, and I have agreed to go with him. He hasn't told her that he is bringing me. She thinks that she will be interviewing him for her new book.

"An ambush," said Anna, her eyes gleaming.

"Yes," said Ling Ti. "I think it will be best to surprise her. The main thing will be to get the Book back."

"What if she doesn't have the Book?" I asked. This is my greatest fear: I have no reason to think that she will have it with her. She might even have sold it.

"If she doesn't have it, she can tell you where it is," said Yuri.

"If I were her, I'd just deny everything," said Icana, frowning. "You can't prove that she took it, or that she has it."

The thought of Jane Watson denying her crime made me cold with rage. "If she does, Ling Ti should write about it, and put it in his magazine," I said. "Everyone must know what she did. And we should tell the university that she ought to be thrown out. I think that she should be exposed as a fraud, even if she gives the Book back to me."

"There's a problem, though," said Ling Ti, glancing quickly at me. "Jane Watson isn't actually a fraud. She's important, Sim. You read her book about the River people. Even you have to admit that it matters. Nobody else is writing about the things she is, and her books make people take notice, especially overseas."

I sat mutinously silent. Ling Ti and I had been having this argument for days. Ling Ti reads dozens of journals and papers, including foreign ones, and is very well informed. He keeps telling me that I should read more.

Patiently, Ling Ti ran through his arguments. He said that Jane Watson's visit to the university was already controversial, because her books had made her powerful enemies. If those people could find a way of disgracing her, they would be delighted. He said that making a scandal would only play into the hands of the people who wanted to silence her. "Do you want to help them, Sim?" he said. "Because, if you destroyed Jane Watson, that's exactly what you would be doing."

"I want her to be punished for what she did," I said. I knew I was right. But Ling Ti was also right, and underneath I knew that, too.

"She might be feeling bad about it, and want to give the Book back anyway," said Anna. "She might be relieved if you ask for it."

"If she does feel bad, why hasn't she given it back already?" I said. "She's had plenty of time."

"Perhaps you could threaten her," said Yuri. "You know, if she won't admit it. Perhaps you could tell her that you will expose her as a thief, and make her give you the Book that way."

"In the end, it's up to you," said Icana. "The wrong is yours."

"Yes," I said. "The wrong is mine."

# 3 4

So I went to see Jane Watson. That was two days ago, and I have been thinking about it ever since.

I was very nervous. I took the day off work and Ling Ti picked me up from my flat after lunch. I had spent the entire morning trying to decide what to wear. It's not as if I had much choice: I don't own many clothes. In the end, I wore a plain black pencil skirt and a white shirt. I put on the gold earrings my grandmother gave me when I was presented at the temple, and I braided my hair, which is now almost as long as it was when I lived in the village. I wanted to look stern and smart and important, like someone it wouldn't be easy to dismiss.

We hardly spoke on the way: I think Ling Ti was almost as nervous as I was. We took the tram to the university. I had never been there before, but Ling Ti knew it well, as he studied there for a year before he left to become a great poet. Inside one of the big new buildings we caught a lift up to the seventh floor and came out into a green-painted corridor lined with numbered doors.

"We want number twenty-three," said Ling Ti.

It didn't take long to find it. We stood in front of the door for a few moments, as if we were preparing ourselves for an ordeal. Then Ling Ti winked at me. Although my heart was hammering in my chest, he made me smile. He raised his fist and knocked on the door, and I heard Jane Watson's voice calling for us to come in.

It was a small, stuffy room, just big enough to hold an enormous desk that was piled with papers, with a tiny window that looked out on a ventilator shaft. The walls were lined with shelves that held stacks of books and files. Jane Watson was standing behind her desk to greet Ling Ti. She was smartly dressed in a woollen suit, but otherwise looked much the same as when I had last seen her, although there were deep circles under her eyes. She gave me a surprised glance, and then turned to Ling Ti and gave him a wide smile.

It felt too ordinary. After all the years of searching, after all the pain and loss, there should have been thunder and lightning. Ling Ti and I should have burst through the door like warriors, brandishing swords over our heads. Jane Watson should have cowered before us and begged for mercy. Instead we crowded awkwardly into a shabby room that was scarcely big enough to hold the three of us.

Jane Watson didn't even recognize me. She thought so little of what she had done that she didn't even remember my face. That's when I lost my temper, silently inside, as if a switch had been flicked on.

"Ling Ti," Jane Watson said, in her language. "What a great pleasure."

"A great pleasure to meet you too," said Ling Ti. "I hope you don't mind, but I brought a friend. She wants to ask you some questions."

Jane Watson frowned. "I was hoping to interview you, and

I don't have a lot of time," she said. "But I suppose that's OK."

"I think you've met her before," said Ling Ti, stepping aside.

This was my cue, and I stepped forward, holding my hand out in greeting. Jane Watson took my hand, looking puzzled. "I don't recall…"

"This is Simbala Da Kulafir Atan Mucarek Abaral Effenda Nuum," said Ling Ti.

"Hello, Jane Watson," I said in my language. My voice was shaking, not with nervousness now but with anger. "I am the Keeper, and you stole my Book."

Jane Watson recognized me at last. She looked shocked, and then a deep blush rose up from her neck, until her whole face was red. She sat down slowly in her chair, staring at me.

"I don't know what you're talking about," she said. She turned to Ling Ti and spoke in her language again. "I don't know why you've…"

A great disgust rose up in my throat at her denial. "Jane Watson," I said, "I remember when you came to my village, and stayed with my family and ate our bread and salt. We trusted you. And then you stole our most precious thing. You stole the Book that belonged to me and my mother and my grandmother and all my mothers before me. It doesn't belong to you, it belongs to us, and I have come to take it back."

While I talked, Jane Watson's face returned to its normal colour. She looked me straight in the eye and said again that she had no idea what I was talking about, and she reached for the phone on the desk. Very gently, Ling Ti took her hand and lifted it away.

"Miss Watson," he said. "Don't call security. Let's not make a scandal. Please don't insult us by pretending that you don't know what we're talking about. If you don't return the Book to its Keeper, I will write about it and everyone will know what you have done. What will that do to your career? Imagine what people will say. The great defender of the River people, a cultural vandal and thief!"

There was a long silence. Jane Watson had now turned very pale. She licked her lips, like a nervous lizard.

"I'm surprised to find that even you are a lackey of the powerful, Ling Ti," she said. "I thought better of you."

"You know very well that I am not."

"And yet you are prepared to smear me."

"I think the newspapers will be very interested," said Ling Ti softly. "After all, they're looking for dirt on you, aren't they? And what will the university say, after sticking its necks out for you? It won't be very happy."

By now I was so angry my hands were shaking. "I don't know how you can sit there and say to my face that you didn't take the Book," I said. "I know you did it. Everyone in my village knows it."

"You can't prove anything," Jane Watson said quickly, and then she bit her lip, aware that she had given herself away.

"Why can't we prove anything?" I said. "Because you stole from people who are less important than you? Because we're not famous and don't write books? What makes you think nobody will listen to us?"

Jane Watson was staring at her desk. Suddenly, to my surprise, I pitied her: she looked small and ashamed.

"And if I give it back?" she said at last.

"If you return it?" said Ling Ti. "We will say nothing."

"Maybe," I said. I was breathing hard. "Maybe we'll say nothing."

There was another long silence. Then Jane Watson stood up and went to a filing cabinet in the corner of the room. She took out a cardboard box and opened it. Inside was the Book. I cried out and snatched it from her.

I knew, straight away, that the Book was dead. It felt like any other book. I opened it with trembling hands, and it fell open on a word that was almost the last thing the Book had said to me. It was in the middle of the page, all by itself. It said: *Change*.

Slowly, carefully, I leafed through the entire book, and every page said the same thing. Only the last pages in the book were different. On them was the answer the Book had given to Jane Watson. There was the drawing of a landscape wound through by a river, and a flock of cranes flying over the horizon. On the facing page was written, in Jane Watson's language: *What profit it a man, if he gains the world and loses his soul?*

I felt a huge bitterness rising up inside me, like a black tide. "You killed the Book," I said to Jane Watson. This time I spoke in her language. "You stole it, and you killed it!"

She said nothing.

"Why? Why did you do it?"

This was the question that had eaten away at me all the time that I was looking for Jane Watson. She sat in her chair, refusing to meet my eye, and I knew then that she wouldn't answer me. I realized I didn't care any more what she had to say. Perhaps even she didn't know why she'd stolen it. She knew it was wrong when she did it, she knew what the Book meant to our village, and she took it anyway. She thought she had the right to take it, because she was a famous writer and we were poor ignorant peasants, with our quaint beliefs and our old-fashioned clothes. She had wanted it, and she had taken it: there was nothing else to say.

"I know what the Book was trying to tell you, now," I said. "I've learned things since I came to the city. The Book was warning you. It even used a verse from your own Holy Book, so you would understand. I bet that was the last thing the Book ever said. I bet you looked inside the Book again before you stole it from our house, and that was what you found. And still you took it."

I stared at Jane Watson with hatred as she sat at her desk, her head bowed. Then she spoke, so quietly I almost couldn't hear her.

"I'm sorry," she said. Then she said it again, in my language.

"It's too late," I said. "And it's not enough."

And then we left.

# 35

I don't want to punish Jane Watson any more. Ling Ti and I have had some fierce arguments about it. I wanted him to write that editorial, I wanted her to be humiliated and exposed, I wanted to be revenged for what she had done to me, to my grandmother, to the whole village. But one day I remembered something my grandmother often said: "Revenge digs two graves." My desire for revenge was corroding my own soul. Punishing Jane Watson won't bring the Book back to life, and it won't make me feel any better.

I haven't forgiven Jane Watson, but Ling Ti is correct: she is more useful as an ally than as an enemy and, although she has done so much harm, she also does some good. "It may be that we have to speak in the enemy's language, if we want to be heard," he said.

Ling Ti often talks like that, as if he were a soldier in a war. I don't want to be part of any war: but, as Ling Ti says, sometimes you have to fight, whether you want to or not.

Life is always more complicated than I would like it to be.

When I think of Jane Watson sitting in her cramped office, looking crushed and ashamed, I am almost certain I don't hate her. When I think of the suffering she has caused me and the people I love, I am almost certain that I do. Perhaps some good will come of this; perhaps Jane Watson will learn how to listen to the people that she says she wants to help. Perhaps one day, if I find I am ready to, I might even forgive her.

Next week, Ling Ti and I will begin the journey with Mizan back to my village. We will stay the whole summer and return to the city in autumn. It has been very complicated to arrange, mainly because of Mely. At first she wanted to come, and then she didn't. At last, after a lot of discussion, we all decided that she would stay with Yuri while I was away, and then she changed her mind again. She hates being cold and damp and uncomfortable, and she remembers our journey to the city with distaste, but she doesn't want to be separated from me. When she told me this, I wanted to cry: she is a very proud cat. To my surprise, she hasn't once objected to my leaving: I thought she would be very angry. But she understands why I must go.

I am longing to see my family again. It's as if I haven't been able to admit quite how much I miss them, and now that we are actually going back to my village, all that missing has rushed in like a flood. I can't wait to talk to my grandmother, and to see my father and sisters and brothers. I wonder how much they have changed in the years I have been away, and what they are doing now. I am planning to visit Shiha to see her twins, and perhaps she will play my mother's favourite song on the *tar* and it will be, for a little while, as if I never left.

Yet I know it will be a sad return, because the Book is no

longer what it was. I feel that I am bringing home a corpse to a grieving family. I have bought a special waterproof box and packed the Book carefully in silk, so it will be safe during our journey. My one hope is that my grandmother will know how to bring the Book back to life. She is very wise and knows more than I do about the Keeping. Perhaps, when it is back home on its special shelf in its room, I will again feel that faint tingle in my fingers, and the Book will remember all the things it knows, the songs and pictures and poems and stories and recipes, the histories and lists and languages. Somewhere in those fragrant pages is the picture of my mother showing me the Book for the first time, and somewhere, as yet unseen, is a picture of Ling Ti. When I looked in the Book for myself, it always showed me what I loved.

Today Ling Ti and Mely and I went to hear Blind Harim the Storyteller. It was a warm day, but heavily overcast: it will thunder later. The market was busy with all the usual traders, and Harim had a large audience. We sat down and waited with everybody else as the small boy brought Harim to his tree, and he raised his voice and began.

He told a very old story that I once read in the Book. It's the story of Yntara, the Mother of All Things, and how she saved us all. I can't tell it as well as he did, because I have neither his bewitching voice nor his skill with words, but it goes like this. In the morning of the world, the god of fire and the god of water were bitter rivals. Over time this turned into hatred, and at last they swore enmity and made ruinous war on each other. The war raged for many years, and fire and water detest each other even to this very day.

In the end the god of water was defeated when the god of fire caused the Great Mountain that held up the whole sky to fall in an avalanche upon his armies. But when the

Great Mountain was destroyed it left an enormous hole in the heavens, and the sky began to fall down onto the earth. Burning stars exploded in the plains and earthquakes felled whole cities, and there was enormous suffering among all the peoples on the surface of the earth.

Yntara heard the cries of her children, and came to help. She tried to mend the hole with many-coloured pebbles she took from the bottom of the River, piling them high and weaving them together with powerful spells, but time after time they tumbled down into rubble. When she saw that she couldn't build a mountain out of pebbles, Yntara stood where the Great Mountain had been and made the most powerful spell there ever was. She turned her body into rock; her raiment became the clouds and mists; and her long hair became the four rivers that flow down each of her sides. And so the sky was mended, and the people of the earth were saved from the destruction of the gods.

The story made me feel hopeful. Perhaps, I said, if we work hard enough, even our ruined world can be healed. I know from Jane Watson's book that if they are treated well, rivers can be restored. Perhaps our River will not die. Perhaps the Book will speak again. Ling Ti said the story was designed to make people feel hopeful, but that it was a delusory hope, and that we couldn't wait for the gods to save us. He said we have to fight for what we love because otherwise it will be stolen from us, and maybe it might cost us our whole lives. Mely said she didn't care what it meant, because it was just a beautiful story.

We squabbled amicably as we wandered through the alleys and streets on the way back to my flat. Then I looked up and saw a flock of cranes, flying high over the city, and pointed them out to Ling Ti. He put his arm around my shoulders and whispered the poem in my ear:

*Watch for the cranes, who will bring my love to you, even as far as the Plains of Pembar.*

Even as far as the Plains of Pembar. Even as far as the city, which is my home.

**ALISON CROGGON** is the acclaimed author of the Books of Pellinor and *Black Spring*, which was a Notable Book in the 2013 Children's Book Council of Australia, Book of the Year Awards and was shortlisted for the 2014 NSW Premier's Literary Awards. She is an award-winning poet whose work has been published extensively in anthologies and magazines internationally. She has written widely for theatre, and her opera libretti have been produced all around Australia. Alison is also an editor and critic. She lives in Melbourne with her husband, the playwright Daniel Keene.

For more information about Alison,
visit: www.alisoncroggon.com
or follow her on Twitter: @alisoncroggon

## Amnesty International

The story of *The River and the Book* has human rights at its very core. The theft of the Book is an abuse of the rights to privacy, culture and property; the destruction of the River and the communities who live along its banks comes about because of business and state abuse of human rights.

We all have human rights, no matter who we are or where we live. The Universal Declaration of Human Rights (UDHR) was adopted in 1948, after the horrors of World War II. It was the first document to agree common, global terms for truth, justice and equality. Human rights help us to live lives that are fair and truthful, free from abuse, fear and want and respectful of other people's rights. But they are often abused and we need to stand up for them, for ourselves and for other people.

Amnesty International is a movement of ordinary people from across the world standing up for humanity and human rights. Our purpose is to protect individuals wherever justice, fairness, freedom and truth are denied.

If you are interested in taking action on human rights, you can find out how to join our network of active Amnesty youth groups at www.amnesty.org.uk/youth

If you are a teacher, take a look at Amnesty's many free resources for schools, including our "Using Fiction to Teach About Human Rights" classroom notes on a range of novels with human rights themes. www.amnesty.org.uk/education

Amnesty International UK, The Human Rights Action Centre
17–15 New Inn Yard, London EC2A 3EA
020 7033 1500
sct@amnesty.org.uk
www.amnesty.org.uk

ALSO BY ALISON CROGGON

# BLACK SPRING

A wild, passionate story of possessive desire and
destructive longing, inspired by the timeless classic
WUTHERING HEIGHTS.

Lina is enchanting, vibrant but wilful.
And her eyes betray her for what she truly is – a witch.
With her childhood companion, Damek, she has grown
up privileged and spoiled, and the pair are devoted to
each other to the point of obsession.
But times are changing.
Vendetta is coming.
And tragedy is stalking the halls of the Red House.

# THE BOOKS OF
# PELLINOR

BOOK ONE
## *THE GIFT*

BOOK TWO
## *THE RIDDLE*

BOOK THREE
## *THE CROW*

BOOK FOUR
## *THE SINGING*

"An epic fantasy in the Tolkien tradition ...
I couldn't put it down!" Tamora Pierce

"A tale with passion, inspiring characters, an enchanting
protagonist and vividly described landscapes ...
will delight fans of Garth Nix and G.P. Taylor."
*The Bookseller*